THEORY OF INDIAN MUSIC

(The first book Containing the sentiments, their effects on shrutis, notes and ragas in ornamental shape along with formation and manner of display)

RAM AVTAR 'VIR'

Sangeetacharya

PANKAJ PUBLICATIONS
NEW DELHI

© RAM AVTAR 'VIR'

Revised Edition 1999

ISBN 81-87155-18-3

Published by :
Pankaj Publications
M-114, Vikas Puri
New Delhi-110018

Distributed by :-
Cambridge Book Depot
3,Regal Building,Sansad Marg,
New Delhi-110001
Phone : 3363395
Fax : 91-11-5163525
E.mail :Cambridgebooks@hotmail.Com

Printed at :
VARDHMAN OFFSET
Delhi-32, © 2059396

PANKAJ PUBLICATIONS

PREFACE

The Indian classical Music owes its origin in vedic period but the reliable facts are obtained from Bharat Natya Shastra written by Bharat Muni in 5th Century A.D. From 5th century A.D. to 13th century A.D. for about seven hundred years the musical activities remained at stand still. In thirteenth century A.D. Sangeet Ratnakar, the second reliable book was written by Pt. Sharang Deva. Both these granthas are considered as the basic informative writings on classical music. From 12th and 13th centuries onwards the muslim rulers reshaped Indian Classical Music through Rag-Ragini system by providing a place to the musicians in their courts. This system continued upto 20th century A.D.

If we study the historical evolution of Indian classical music, we would come to know that the period of seven or eight hundred years i.e. from 12th century A.D. to 20. century A.D. is the time of optimum progress of music. The musical programmes in Royal courts were performed not only for entertainments but they were also displayed, to make the Emperor jolly and peaceful minded so that he may give true and merciful judgement. The sentiments of forgiveness and mercy evolve out of sweet and impressive music. This idea is supported by historical facts.

Some authors hold the opinion that musical activities come to greatest retoriation in this period as the common people started to hate music but in my opinion it is far from reality as they are seen in prosperous condition in this period. The Hindu and Muslim rulers of this period held the musicians in high regard and spent a lot of money over them.

So far as the hatred towards music is concerned, it might be due to the fact that the musical programmes were performed for the entertainment of victorious armies. The young musicians both male and female were forcefully made to sing and dance. This system of forceful musical display was not liked by the common people so started to hate them.

When Muslim rule came to an end and the Europeans took over the charge of administration, the court musicians started to impart musical education and were called as Gharanas but the singers and the dancers of army were not accepted and honoured by the common people.

Pt. Vishnu Narayan Bhat Khande in his collection of classical songs in form of exhaustive granta—Kramik Pustika in 6 volumes supports the fact that the musicians of medieval age were held in high regards by the rulers of that age and the modern music is the result of their efforts.

Having considered over music and the musical activities Pt. Vishnu Digamber Paluskar laid foundation of Gandharva Mahavidyalaya in Lahore (now in Pakistan) in 1901 and started to impart education through his own notation system but on account of presence of various Gharanas spread over India, the method of instructions of teaching music was different due to difference in prolongation, ascent and descent and manner of singing. Having seen such diverse circumstances in musical activities the royal families and the educated society of the country took interest for the unification of music.

The first All-India Music Conference, convened in 1916 by H.H. the Maharaja Gaekwar of Baroda, inaugurated several projects of reform, as will be seen by the following memoradum.

AUTHOR'S GRATITUDE

I am pleased to present this volume 'The Theory of Indian Music, in hands of needy readers on the mercy of All Mighty God who awakened my beings with his deep hidden touches and provided with inspiration and power to my pen to write this book in English language.

My deepest obligations are to the authors of following Books :

Sanskrit & Hindi books : Rig Veda, Sam Veda, Bharat Natya Shastra, Laghu Sidhant Kaumudi, Sangeet Ratnakar, Sangeet, Parijata, Sangeet Darpan, Sangeet Sar-Amrit Udchar, Rag Chandrika Sar, Rag Kaldrumankur, Chatvarichcha Rag nirupanam, Swar mel kala Nidhi, Chatur Dandik Prakashika, Vedic Swar meemansa, Patanjal Yog Darshan, Sri Madbhagwat Geeta, Hindustani Sangeet paddhati and Kromic Pustak Malika (in 6 volumes).

English:—Music of India, Story of Indian Music and its Instruments, Theory of Indian Music, three Monographs on music, A short historical survey of music of Upper India, A comparative study of some of the leading music systems and Sangeet of India.

Urdu—Sharma-e-Isharat, Tahseel-ul-Sitar, Nad Viond Grantha, Ainae Mosike, Kanoon Rag Music of India and Tafseel-ul-Mosike.

I also wish to acknowledge with deep gratitude the large help I have received from Pandit Vinaya Chandra Maudgalya, the Principal Gandharva Mahavidyalaya, New Delhi, Khan Saheb Hafiz Ahmad Khan, Dy. Programme Director, All India Radio New Delhi, Pandit Ved Parkash Shastri, D-MA Sidhanlinkr, Sri Ishwari Prasad Gupta M.A., the Author of many English and Hindi Educational and General Books, Srimati Tara Ramaswamy the Principal Delhi Institute of Music and Dance and Sri Inder Mani the Publisher of this book .

Ram Avtar Veer

The aims and objects of the All-India Music Conference, as setted at Baroda in 1916 are as follow :

1. To take steps to protect and to make uplift of our Indian music on national lines.

2. To reduce the same to a regular system such as would be easily taught to and learnt by our educated country men and women.

3. To provide a fairly workable unfirom system of ragas and talas (with special reference to the northern system of music).

4. To effect if possible such a happy fusion of the northern and sourthern systems of music as would enrich both.

5. To provide a uniform system of notation for the whole country.

6. To arrange new raga productions on scientific and systematic lines.

7. To consider and take further steps towards the improvement of our musical iustruments, under the light of our knowledge of modern science, all the while taking care to preserve our nationality.

8. To take steps to correct and preserve permanently the great masterpieces of this sublime art now in the possession of our first-class artists and others.

9. To collect in a great central library all available literature (ancient and modern) on the subject of Indian music, and if necessary, to publish it and render it available to our students of music.

10. To examine and fix the microtones of shrutis of Indian music with the help of our scientific instruments, and the first-class recognised artists of the day, and to make an attempt if possible to distribute them among the ragas.

11. To start an "Indian Men of Music" series.

12. To conduct a monthly journal of music on up-to-date lines.

13. To raise a permanent fund for carrying on the above-mentioned objects.

14. To establish a National Academy of Music in a central place where first-class instruction in music could be given on most up-to-date lines by eminent scholars and artists in music.

As a result of the All India Music Conferences academies and colleges were established in various parts of India and schemes were afloat for the creation of musical faculties at Indian Universities. In 1919 an All India Music Academy was inaugurated for the collection of classical music, the systematisation of Ragas and melodies, the foundation of music library etc.

In 1925 the Fourth All India Music Conference was held in Lucknow under the Presidentship of his excellency, Sir William Sinclair Marris, the Governor of U.P. He founded Marris Music College at Lucknow which is running as Bhatkhande Music University at present.

Gandharva Mahavidyalaya had already been established in Bombay by that time. Ethel Rosenthel the author of story of Indian Music and its Instrument's has written about Gandharva Mahavidyalaya at Bombay as follows:

"Interest in music was awakened recently in Gujarat, and a musical conference was held in November, 1926, at Ahmedabad, under the auspices of the Gandharva Mahavidyalaya of Bombay, one of the leading academies of Indian music. It was a sign of the emancipation of women that an Indian lady, Mrs. Vidyagauri Ramanbhai, should have been elected as president. She performed her offices most efficiently and dwelt upon the importance of music as an educational factor. Pandit Vishnu Digamber, Principal of the Bombay Music School, mentioned that music had been cultivated in Gujarat in past ages, and expressed the hope that before very long, every Indian child would learn music. Several concerts and competitons took place in connection with the conference."

The two popular and recognised systems of imparting education were Gandharva Mahavidyalaya and V. N. Bhatkhavde in India. The theory as a whole is taught through Bhatkhande system in schools and colleges. The music is playing an appreciable role on Radios, Televisions and film Industry but the common people and the young generation has not yet been much benefited by the classical music so far. The music theory is holding responsibility of this lackness of interest and knowledge because our music theory fails to explain the form of Ragas and the origin of Rasas in them so that the beginners may display them correctly. Besides there is no such instrument which may show the sound of shrutis and may be helpful to the beginners and the young children in prolongation of Ragas.

I have taken old and popular 24 shrutis in place of 22, and have also established notes on old scale system so that one may be benifitted with the sentiments of notes and shrutis. I have shown in details the outlines of sentiments, their movement and effect on notes alongwith formation and method of singing of Ragas.

The movement of sentiments in Ragas has been illustrated with pictures in other publication of mine—Raga Asavary which deals with Dhrupad, Dhamar and Khyals of Rag Asavary, Jaunpury, Darbary, Adana and Gandhary in combined notation which has been drownout by the combination of staff music notation and Indian music notation.

I hope this book will be a great help to the Indian as well as foreign musicians.

Short comings if any will be welcomed for correction in further editions.

Veeranwali Bhawan
M-24 Kirti Nagar
New Delhi-110015.

Ram Avtar Vir
Sangeet Acharya

CONTENTS

What is Music ?

The morning Will Surely come, the darkness will vanish, and the voice pour down in golden streams breaking through the sky.

When thy words will take wings in Songs from every one of my brid's nests, and thy melodies will break forth in flowers in all my forest groves.

—Rabindra Nath Tagore

Such were the views of great music lover and expert Sri Rabindra Nath Tagore who regarded music as a source of delight as well as a source of uniting natural phenomena to soul or God making 'Love is God and God is music' a meaningful phrase.

Music is present in every living and non living beings—men, animals, birds, fountains rivers, winds, and even in trees which produce the natural sound in sweet rhythmical way. The Source of musical rhythm is the Nada.

Anahat nada is the source of music and when some ideas evolve out through one's throat in rhythmical and appealing sound they take the form of Ahat nada which we call musical sound. When Ahat nada is sung in proper time and rhythm it appeals the human heart as every living being possesses the musical instincts. Music in its true shape controls the human activities—Kama, Krodha, Lobha, Moha and Ahankara etc., and overall maintains the equilibrium of his mind. Music in this way is the source of achieving complete pleasure and attaining salvation.

It creates social instincts i.e. feelings of love and sympathy towards human beings.

Before the Vedic age when there was no language to express the feelings of heart, music was the source of keeping the family life healthy when the early people at the night time assembled at a place and enjoyed themselves by singing and dancing they felt relief in their whole day exhausion and enjoyed sound sleep at night.

In Vedic age man found out the way of expression through vowels and Sanskrit language came into existance and Ved mantras were written in epic form, called chhandas or Shrutis. The Rishis, who used to pronounce the Ved mantras through Udatta, Anudatta and Swarit, were given due honour. These rishis expressed the ascent and descent of sound through waving of hands so that they may pronounce the mantras in proper time and rhythm.

This practice is still repeated by the music directors. Music at that time was the source uniting human soul with God which we call salvation.

After this music found its place in the Court of Indra where the singer was called as Gandharva, the instrument player as Kinnar and the dancer as the Apsara. All the Rishi-Munis including Shanker and Narada used to sing and dance. After that the musicians separated them selves from common people and became a source of religious preaching which started Deva dasi system and the musicians were called kathaks.

In medieval age Gandharvas were named as Gayaks, Kinnars as Vadaks and Apsaras and Nratraks.

When Britishers came in India and started to rule over the country Sir William John was the first English man to express his views about Indian Music.

View of some English writers about Indian music

Music appeals to people everywhere and has been at the heart of all human societies. In the stone Age society of the Australian Aborigines and the refined artificiality of ancient imperial China in the elegance of 18th century Europe and the fast—moving and complex world of today, music has attended on ceremony and religion, has given entertainment and has been a source of deep inspiration.

—*The Larousse Encyclopedia of Music*
Edited by Geoffrey Hindley.

ON THE MUSICAL MODES OF THE HINDUS

The following treatise on Indian Music by Sir William Jones (1746-94) is reproduced from the third volume of 'Asiatic Researches', 1799, a rare work, described on the title-page as the "Transactions of the Society instituted in Bengal for inquiring into the History and Antiquities, the Arts, Sicences and Literature of Asia.

Sir William Jones founded the Asiatic Society in 1784, shortly after his arrival in Calcutta. He was a great scholar and remarkable linguist, possessing a thorough knowledge of thirteen languages. He was acquainted with the theory of music, and his essay is one of the earliest and most interesting contributions by an English writer to the study of Indian music.

A reprint of the treatise is included in "Hindu Music from various Authors", compiled by Raja Comm. Sourindro Mohun Tagore, Calcutta, 1882.

MUSICK belongs, as a Science, to an interesting part of natural philosophy, which by mathematical deductions from constant phenomena, explains the causes and properties of sound, limits the number of mixed, or harmonick, sound to a certain series, which perpetually recurs, and fixed the ratio, which they bear to each other, or to one leading term; but, considered as an Art, it combines the sounds, which philosophy distingnishes in such a manner as to gratify our ears, or affect our imaginations, or, by uniting both objects, to captivate the fancy while it pleases the sense, and speaking, as it were, the language of beautiful nature, to raise correspondent ideas and emotions in the mind of the hearer; it then, and then be comes what we call a fine art, allied very nearly to verse, painting and rhetorick, but subordinate in its functions to pathetick poetry, and inferior in its power to genuine eloquence

—Written in 1784, and since much
Enlarged by the Author

The Hindu mythology the various departments of life and learning are usually associated with different rishis and so to one of these is traced the first instruction that men received in the art of music. Bharata rishi is said to have taught the art to the heavenly dancers—the Apsaras—who afterwards performed before Siva. The rishi Narada, who wanders about in earth and heaven, singing and playing on his vina, taught music to men. Among the inhabitants of Indra's heaven we find bands of musicians. The Gandharvas are the singers, the Apsaras the dancers, and the Kinnars centaur-like performers on musical instruments. From the name Gandharva has come that title **Gandharva Veda** for the art of music.

—The Music of India
by Herbert A. Popley

The Indian word for music is Sangita, which means a chorus or a song sung by many voices, and also applies to singing accompanied by playing of instruments and dancing. In its vast compass, therefore, Indian music includes music in all its forms, vocal, instrumental, oral, together with the allied arts of dancing and gesticulating. As in all other advanced countries so in India, music is considered to be a fine art. As such it may be defined as an art which employs sounds (not necessarily words), combined so as to be agreeable to the ear, as a medium of expressing one's emotions and perceptions, and of creating in the hearers the emotions, and perceptions desired by the artists. It is the finest among the fine arts.

—Theory of India Music
by Swarup

SANGIT, is formed of Surs (tones), and Tals (times). Each is dependent upon the other for a complete sympathetic arrangement for a final expression of Gayan (singing), Vadan (playing), and Nritya (dancing). All creations in nature have sounds. Some are positive, and loud, and can be heard distinctly without paying special attention to them like thunder, the roaring of the sea, the bellowing of a buffalo; there are other sounds that are definite, and have to be listened to with attention, like the singing of the birds, the whispering of the winds, and the trickle of water; then there are the third kind of sounds that are inner, and have to be perceived by developing the hidden subtle sense of hearing, like the movement of the stars, the vibrations in the atmosphere, and an unexpressed melody-unidentified. These 3 kinds of sound were defined by the ancients and determined into Surs, Surats, and Srutis forming a comprehensive scale, as the foundation of music.

— Sangeet of India
by Ateya Begum

The music to day is considered as an Art and the musicians as an Artist making music as profession to earn his living.

11

Sangeet is not an Art

Sangeet is a medium of expressing the feelings of human pleasures and calamities. It is the best ornament and is awarded by nature to few. We weep when we face some calamity and our heart leaps with joy and begins to sing and dance when hears some happy news. Art is limited to human beings only but sangeet is an interesting part of natural philosophy which explains causes and properties of sound. It affects the animals, birds and plant life. Under the pleasure giving atmosphere of sangeet the milk animals like cows over pour more milk. The musicians of medieval age have successfully proved that the elephant starts to dance on the sound of Mradang and Pakhavaj while a deer comes to the hunter when over joyed on Rag Todi. The snake swings its hood on the sweet and charming voice of Bean. The great musician Tan Sen Performed an experiment for the removal of diseases through music. Even to day a sick man feels a great relief when sweet and charming songs are sung before him. Under such circumstances sangeet can not be called as an Art.

Art can only be the means of recreation to others. It does not affect the human beings permanently. We listen different kinds of songs and forget them afterwards. Sangeet in real shape is the best gift to man. It is a source of approaching God and can be possible by a constant practice.

2

Outlines of Indian Music History

"History is the narration of memorable past events. It gives the knowledge of glorious culture and civilization of man and his society. History is such a wide subject that it knows no beginning or end. Each act of historical episode is the effect of some previous episode and probably leads on to another".—K. A. Nilkantha Shastri and H. S. Ramanna.

One must have the proper concept of facts. The past cannot be constructed by man whose knowledge of life has been gained only from documents. Mere documentation of facts is not enough.

The character of a nation is the history of its past and to understand it, we have to turn on the lime light of the history of its people through Art, since it is related to culture. The higher the fine Arts of a people or nation, the higher is its cultural level. Music is known as a fine art at present and hence history of music shall be known as art of arts.

History of music is closely related to the human society from the very beginning of creation. It does not ignore the imaginative and creative faculties of man. Every nation or society made their music a means of progress and prosperity of social, political, cultural, religious and spiritual values of life. In the remote days all rites and ceremonies were closely connected with music. In India Music formed an integral and indispensable part of life.

The history of Indian music has extruded itself from the prehistoric age to the present time. It has evolved an inevitable material for the changing circumstances of human society. Regarding evolutional and progressive nature of art of music Cecil Gray writes, in the history of music, "In no art, science or other departments of human activity, has the doctrine of evolution been so enthusiastically welcomed, so eagerly adopted and so whole heartedly adorned as in music. The gradual progress of Indian music is really a key to the whole range of musical production that flowed from the imaginative conception of the Indian people.

Music started from the very original voices of a—e—i—o—u etc. produced by man at the time of his birth. Even today the first cry of the new born human babe is from such a basic sound at the first moment of awareness to the world. These original voices are converted into sounds of music afterwords.

13

The formation of consonants was also done on the basis of the position of our throat connected by the two chords in the voice by sound. These vowels and consonents are noted below :

Vowel	Position of Origin	Vowel	Position or Origin.
-a	Throat	e	Throat & Pollette
-aa	Throat	ai	Throat & Pollette
-i	Pollette	o	Throat & lips
-ee	Pollette	au	Throat & lips
u	Lips	ah	Throat
oo	Lips		

The Scheme of Transliteration of Consonents

Gutturals	k	kh	g	gh	n	
Palatals	ch	chh	j	jh	n	s'
Linguals	t	th	d	dh	n	sh
Dentals	t	th	d	dh	n	s
Libials	p	ph	b	bh	m	
	y	r	l	v	h	

History of Indian Music is divided into following evolutionary periods :

(i) *Aryan Period :* Starting from Vedic times to tenth century A.D.

(ii) *Muslim Period :* Starting from Eleventh Century A.D. to Eighteenth Century A.D.

(iii) *English Period :* Starting from early Eighteenth Century to the achievement of Independence.

(iv) *Period of Independent India* After independence upto present time.

Aryan Period

In Vedic period when work of writing the Ved Mantras was started for the first time, the Swaras (Vowels) which came out of the mouth spontaneously, were taken as the base. These Swaras were taken from old Sanskrit language.

The Vedic Richas or the Ved Mantras are also called the 'Shrutis'. The notation system which was adopted to sing them is given below :

In Vedic period, the Ved Mantras were recited in Epic form and the ascent and discent of those mantras were done on the directions of special sign. These signs were :

(i) Udat   (ii) Anudat   (iii) Swarit

Udat : A note recited in high pitch is called Udat. It is symbolized by a small Vertical line marked over the note which is to be pronounced in high pitch.

14

Anudat : A note recited in low pitch is called Anudat. It is symbolized by a horizontal line marked under the note to be pronounced in low pitch. The horizontal line has been shown as the sign of Anudat in Rig Ved. (Kashmiri Path). Yajurved and Athrvved.

Swarit : Swarit note denotes the combination of Udat and Anudat. It is expressed without any sign.

In Sam Ved Udat sound is expressed by writing the figures over the note instead of above the signs of vertical and horizontal lines.

Note : Some scholars of the Vedas differ in opinion about the use of horizontal lines over the notes. To avoid this matter of difference of opinion, we have used the signs on the basis of sound.

In "Vedic Vangbhasya", the word Swara has been used specially for Vowels Dharma of the grammar of the Ved. The Signs Udat and Anudat used on the Swaras (Vowels). These signs were used for only the sound.

"Patanjali" has written that the position of our throat for pronouncing these note signs in three parts i.e. "Udat" is pronounced from the upper part, "Swarit" from the middle and "Anudat" from the lower one. This division should not be taken as the Octave.

Historical facts prove that Swarit is sung with the combination of Udat and Anudat. It contains half matra of Udat and the remaining one and a half matra of Anudat.

Ved Gayans are mainly sung in Swarit. The Udat and Anudat signs are used on Vowels for high and low pitch. In music when we pronounce Swaras, our sound remains fixed but when we pronounce words, it moves up and down. Hence, the sound of Swarit expresses itself in combination with the Shrutis of Udat and Anudat.

Swaras are those which explain the 'Padas'. Besides the above the following Swaras have also been mentioned in the Vedas :

Kampan Swara

In the absence of Udat and Swarit, Jatya, Kshepra, Prashlesh and Abhinihit Swarit are pronounced by Vibrations.

One Note : In Vedic period one note was categorised in two parts :

(a) Tan Swara   (b) Parvachan Swara

Tan Swara was used in other Brahman Granthas.

In Vatsanaya Pratishakhya also 1/131/Tan Swara has been used in Sam, Jap and Niynkha Mantras. In converting Mantras of Sanhita Patha into Pad Patha the sign of Stoppage should be given. In pronouncing the first and the second part of the pada, we should have a stoppage (1) of one Matra time.

15

After signs of Swar notes one Shruti sign was added to it and number became four. After is the number of Swar signs became seven as given below :

In Mahabhashya these seven swaras are given as below :

Udata, Udattar, Anudat, Anudattar, Swarit, Udata, used before in Udata and one Shruti.

Bhashin Shootra also explains these swaras. In Tetriya Pratishakhya they are called Krusta, Pratham, Dutiya, Tritiya, Chaturtha, Mandra and Ati Swaria.

The seven swaras are also mentioned in Naradeeya Shiksha as Shadaj, Rishabh, Gandhar, Madhyam, Pancham, Dhaivat and Nishada.

The Musical instruments of Vedic age :

1. *Dundubhi*—An ordinary drum.
2. *Adambara*—A kind of drum.
3. *Bhumidundubhi*—An earth drum made by digging a hole in the ground and covering it with hides.
4. *Vanaspati*—A wooden drum.
5. *Aghati*—A symbol used to accompany dancing.
6. *Kandha Beena*—A kind of flute.
7. *Karkari*—Another kind of flute.
8. *Vana*—A lute of 100 strings.
9. *Tanava*—A wooden flute .
10. *Nadi*—A reed flute.

In the Vedic Age the chanters and the common people were content with purely sacred hymnal type of samans of Samganas which were possessed of different numbers of note signs. In the beginning of classical period (600 to 500 B.C.) Samganas were replaced by Gandharva type of music which evolved in connection with drama. The Gandharva music was a kind of stage song possessed of Swaras, Talas and Padoo.

This history of Indian music acknowledges that music in India was popular even before the time of Panini. The regular system of notation had been worked out before the age of this grammarian i.e. before 350 B.C. At that time the seven notes were designed by their initial letters. According to Imperial Gazettier of India, the Indian Brahmins brought these notes to Persia and Arabia in 11th century A.D. Thence forward, they were introduced in European music by Guido'd Arezzo in the beginning of 12th century A.D. In this way it is clear that music owes its origin in India and from India, it was introduced to Persia, Arabia and European countries.

In the Epic age, of Ramayana and Mahabharata i.e. from 400 B.C. to 200 A.D. the stories of Ramayana and Mahabharata were sung in musical rhythm. The pronouncers used

Veena Venu and Miradanga etc. to have better performance of their improvisation. In this period of Ramayana and Mahabharata, we see the use of the Seven Notes in musical performances on religious occasions.

RAVANA was proficient performer and allotted a large part of his province to the maintenance of music experts. There is a musical instrument, played in Gujarat, called after his name, Ravanhatta, used by mandicants. The kings were pattrons and artists of music and it formed a part of the early education of Princes. Even the royal ladies cultivated sangitee in their own Sangit Shalas (music slogans), built specially for that purpose and attached to their places. It is said that the 'Bow' had been invented by Ravana.

In the period of Mahabharata, Lord Krishna has been a great politician, Yogi and well versed musician and dancer. He used to play on flute which made the cows and other wild animals spell bound. He also danced in the company of Gopikas at the time of seasonal functions like Hori etc. Arjun also is said to be a great musician. At time of his exile he used to teach dance to the daughter of Raja Pareekshat. In Ramayana Period Lava and Kusha, the sons of Sri Rama, sang the verses written by Rishi Valmiki in the Royal Court of Rama.

The padipadal written in Tamil language, also describes the 22 shruties, seven notes and also categories of Ragas. It shows that Tamilnadu of today had a good quality music in pre Ramayana and Mahabharata age. After this period of great war (Mahabharata) only, a few young people survived and the civilization scattered. History remained silent to produce reliable informations.

GAUTAMA BUDDHA, the noble religious reformer was well versed musician and expounded his doctrines by musical representation and references. Abstemious Buddhists and recluse Jains, too were not indifferent to the charms of music.

ASHVA GHOSHA, who travelled with a party of musicians about the beginning of the Christian era, was the means of converting many persons of distinction by the skill and magic of his performance. In his 'Life of Buddha', he says : "They placed the dead body of Tathagatha, using all kinds of dances and music. To win over the deity, is to sing his praise through prayers."

"Music hath power to make the Heavens descend upon earth" displays the early innate belief in the mythical portrayal of this wonderful sciene (Sangeet of India by Atiya Begem).

In 5th century A.D. Bharata Natya Shastra was written. Rishi Bharata descrices both types of music—Vocal and Instrumental alongwith dancing activities in full details. The author of the book has also clearly described the Shrutis Swaras, Grams and Murchhahas etc. This book is considered to be the basic book on this subject. Jati Gayan was popular at that time.

In times of Bharata Natya Shastra the Jati Gayans were sung. Rag Gayan had not yet come in practice. It came after the times of Bharata i.e. after 3rd Century A.D. But the definition and use of Raga has first of all been given by Matanga Muni in his Brahaddeshi Grantha in 6th Century A.D.

17

In 4th Century the great poet Kalidas wrote several granthas. The verses of these granthas were sung in musical rhythm. The Hindu rulers of that time, gave place to musicians in their darbars. Alongwith the progress of the dramas of the Kalidas, the musical activities also progressed to a considerable extent. Rag Gayan was not yet introduced. That probably came in times of Samudra Gupta in the middle of 5th Century A.D.

In Seventh Century A.D. started the Bhakti Andolan. In this Bhakti period various types of Bhakti Songs were sung by the preachers in musical rhythm with the result that music also progressed side by side. By VIII and IX centuries the progress was little hampered and in the 10th Century A.D. the musical activities took a progressive turn and the most flourishing Indian music has been seen during the period of the Hindu princes. Some of the popular books such as Naradi-Shiksha were also written in this period. This was the time of appreciable prosperity of Indian music in the Hindu period. They were keenly interested in holding of courts and hence music had a chance to achieve a position in the royal families, especially in singing and dancing activities. The theory of music remained at a stand-still.

Muslim Period

The Muslim rulers held the musicians in high esteem. Several new Ragas were originated in this period. There were many musicians in the court of *Mahmood Ghaznavi*, who sang Persian songs. The taste for Kawali style of chanting was also introduced by the Sufis whose religious tendencies inclined towards devotional demonstrations and made them extremely popular both with the Hindus and the Muslims. They came originally from Baghdad and brought into practice the Darvish's ecstatic dance called 'The Whirling Darvishes.

In the reign of Sultan Altamash, the leading exponent Kazi Hamidudden of Nagor got admission to the Royal Court and the Sufi Chisties gave religious sanction. This tended towards popularizing Sufi music at once, and people began to indulge in it unrestrainedly. The intermixing continued with vigour. Sangit Ratnakar was brought out in the reign of Sultan Feroze Shah, son of Altmash, in 1237 adding valuable link to the music of that period.

Sharangdeo wrote Sangeet Ratnakar describing Nada, Shruti, Swaras, Grams, Moorchhas and Jati Gayan etc. in a simple way. This book is considered the basic book on the Indian Music. FEROZE SHAH, collected Persian, Arabian, and Indian Musicians of both sexes and music reigned supreme.

KAIKOBAD, fifty years later come on the throne and stressed the cultivation of music as a compulsory Art, was himself a great patron and performer. Two years later the Khilji dynasty was founded and Jalaludeen Feroze Shah, came on the Masand (throne). In his Durbar flourished the famous exponents :—Mohammad Shah, Fatuha, Changi, Nasir Khan and Bahroz.

In 11th century no musical activity could have a progressive trend, as their commencement brought several unrestful occurrences. But 12th century gave certain appreciable activities in the musical circle. Jaidev, born near Bolpur in Bengal was the first known musician by that time. He wrote the Geeta Gobind containing songs of love between Radha and Krishna.

The musical activities reached its zenith of splendour in the time of Allauddin Khilji in 14th Century A.D. Amir Khusro was a poet-musician and state minister of Allauddin Khilji.

Amir Khusro did appreciable work in the field of music. He invented new Ragas such as Zeelaf, Sajgiri, Sarparda, Yaman, Ratkee Puriya (Night song), Barari, Todi, Todi-Asawary and Puravi, new songs such as Kaul, Kalbana, Tarana, Khayal, (Kavvali Khayal), Naksh, Niggar, Gazal Tillana, and Shola etc., New Talas such as Khamsa, Sawaree, Pahalwan, Jhap, Fardaust, Pasto, Kavvali, Ada—Chautal, Jhumara, Jald-Trital etc. He also invented some musical instruments like Sitar, Tabla and Dhol (Drum). Sitar at the time was named as Sehtar means three stringed instrument. He used in frets in this instrument.

In South India Gopal Nayak, the famous musician of Court of Raja Deva Rai of Vijayanagar invented new Ragas like Budhans, Sarang, Peelu and Biram etc.

SULTAN MOHAMMAD SHAH TUGHLUK, in his glorious reign a most fantastic circular structure called Tarabad was erected in Doultabad. This was embellished by tastefully furnished rooms, all round in the shape of an amphitheatre, with a huge demonstration hall in the centre. In these elegant rooms, open to view, reclined beautiful maidens, on swings surrounded by handmaids in glittering costumes. The Darogha or leader was a Persian nobleman of high extraction, named SHAMASUDDIN TABRIZ. The title of Amir was bestowed on the preceptor, thus pointing to the prestige and status in which music was held in those days. "This elysium of joy" with its most elaborate arrangements was reserved for the entertainment of royal guest, who as a great mark of favour, were located there. Grand variety performances took place, under the able guidance of the Choudhary in the domed hall reserved for the purpose.

The harmoney of Arab-Persian-Hindu music had by this time resulted in many new tunes such as Zeeluf, Nowros, Jangula, Iraq, Yeman, Hooseini, Zilla, Durbari, Hejaz Khamaj, Sarparda etc. These were adopted and sung throughout the empire.

52 names of Talas in vague were : Chou, Panch, Ast, Ganesh, Bhairaon, Chapak, Kooha, Avadat, Shudh, Jya Jewat, Rupak, Durat, Lila, Shrital, Amehlo, Rang, Dareen, Guj Lila, Hans Lila, Sarang Lila, Rangvat, Raj, Sangad, Himali, Ang, Hansnarsing, Jey, Nandan, Kookhla, Deepak, Narthaki, Ram, Sum, Ahinand, Abhinand, Barabor, Bedba, Bir, Kal, Orcha, Phar, Yek, Rajbedh, Surbikrat, Jaymangal, Gandharp, Bikram, Perbat, Rangbhara, Nerat.

In fifteenth century A.D. Sultan Husain Shirqi the ruler of Jaunpore invented Khayal Gayan (Kalavanti Khayal) and also new Ragas such as Jaunpuri, Sindh-Bhairavi, Jaunpore Todi, Raman Todi, and Rasooli Todi etc. and 12 types of shiamas (Gaur Shiam, Malhar Shiam, Basant Shiam and Poorvi Shiam etc.). In the same period, the Bhakti Andolan (Movement) started in northern India. This movement gave momentum to the birth of Sankeertana and Nagar Keertan that came into practice as the religious preachers wandered over the streets singing the Bhakti songs.

In 16th century A.D. Emperor Akbar took a keen interest in music. He kept many well reputed musicians like Tan Sen, Nayak Baiju, Ram Das Raj Bahadur (King of Malwa), Tantarang Khan. Besides there were also some famous musicians like Swami Haridas and and Rani Roopmati etc. Guru of Tansen, Tulsi Das, Surdas and Meera Bai. Akbar himself was familiar with vocal and instrumental music.

Tan Sen was the Court musician of Akbar. He invented new Ragas like Miyan kee Todi, Miyan kee Malhar, and Meyan kee Sarang etc. Nayak Baiju was next to Tansen in importance. He invented Darbari, Lankdhan, Sarang, Dhulia-malhar etc. In the same way Ramdas started Ramdasi Malhar and Swami Haridas Jogiya Raga.

Besides, the Court musicians, there were also some other musicians such as Raja Man Tanwar of Gwalior who is considered the father of Dhrupad Gayan. He was also fond of Shankirna Ragas or mixed modes. It is said that he was very fond of the Sankeeran like Gujaree, Bahut Gujaree, Mal Guzari and Mangal Gujaree. Besides Raja Man Pundareek Vitthal of Burhanpur in South India, was also a prominent musician of 16th Century. He wrote four books like Sarvado Uday Chandrovidaya, Raga Mala, Raga Mangaree and Nartan or Nidayan. He itroduced his own Thatas in 22 already existing Thatas. Raga Mala and Raga Manjaree contained only Northern system of Music while Sadrog Chandreuodaya both North and South Indian music. In the same period Rama Matya wrote Swarmela Kalanidhi containing South Indian system.

After the death of Emperor Akbar in 1605, his son Jahangir became the Emperor of Delhi. He was not a lover of music like his father Akbar. He took no interest in musical activities, even then Jahangeerdad Chhatar Khan, Purvezad and Khurram-dad Makhu, Haurzard Belaokhan were the famous musicians of his court. Two of the most important books of 17th century are Rag Bibodh written by Pt. Somnath of Rajmundri (in 1609) and Sangeet Darpan by Pt. Damodar Mishra (in 1625). Rag Bibodh describes the various types of Veena and the method of playing it while Sangeet Darpan describes the Indian musical system.

In Seventeenth century Shah Jahan, son of Jahangir, became the Emperor of India. He was lover of vocal and instrumental musics. He was well versed in Urdu songs and was much influenced by Sufee melodies that were so enchanting. So he allowed Sufee songs in every evening programme. The famous musicians of his court were, Mahapatten, Jagannath who received the title of Kaviraj, Lal Khan and Dairang Khan (known as Gunsamudsa). The most important book on the system of Indian music published in this period was Sangeet Parijat written by Pt. Ahobal. The author of the book established shuddha and Vikraj Swaras at different lengths of the string. After Sangeet Panjat, Sri Haridaya Narain Deva wrote two books on the subject. These books were Haridaya Kautuk and Haridaya Prakash. Like Ahobal, Sri Haridaya Narain too established the shuddha and Vikrit swaras on different lengths of strings of veena. He used the shuddha thata according to the Kaffee thata of the present days.

In the later half of the seventeenth century there was set back to the prosperity of Indian music. The Emperor Aurangzeb was despotic Mohammadan ruler and hated musical activities and turned out all the musicians from the court and ordered the Police to stop such performances and destroy their musical instruments and bury them so deep into the ground that no musical sound be heared from in future.

But in spite of all these unfavourable activities Pt. Venkata Makhee of South India wrote the Chaturdandi Prakashika in 1660. He popularised the principle that 72 thatas can be formed from 12 Shuddha and Vikrit Swaras on mathematical grounds. In the same period Pt. Bhava Bhatta wrote 3 books—Anoop Vikas, Anupavkash and Anup Sangeet Ratnakara.

The musical performances again sprouted even in the royal courts. Mohammad Shah Rangeela was a great lover of music. Adarang and Sadarang were the two prominent musicians of his court. Both these brothers popularised the Khayal Gayakee and wrote many Khayals and taught them to their pupils. In the same period Ghulam Nabi Shoree started Tappa Gayan.

3

The System of Musical Education in the Medieval Age

Before the Rag-Ragini system of Music many musicians started their schools called Matas. The number of Matas known upto that time was 21 and after the commencement of Rag-Ragini system all these Matas merged into four :—

(a) Shameshwar Mata's Group.

(b) Bharat Mata's Group.

(c) Kalinath Mata's Group.

(d) Hanuman Mata's Group.

These Matas were a kind of school to popularise music according to their own principles. Why the number of Matas given four is a question of dispute as yet. It seems that these four Matas bore their origin after their originator or founder. It also seems that these Matas might have taken their root name after four Mathas established by Sankaracharya. They got the name after the most prominent figure of that area as shown below :—

Name of Matha	Location	Prominent Personality of Area
1. Shrangeri	Present Karnataka	Rishi Bharat
2. Govardhan	Puri	Hanuman
3. Sharda	Dwarika	Lord Krishna
4. Joshi	Badrinath	Lord Shiva

These four Matas continued upto the times of Tansen but after his death his descendents started to work for the uplift of music and the four schools which they made for importing education in music, were considered as four Banis as given below :—

1. *Khandari Bani* was invented by Hussen Khan. It admitted Dhurpad Dhamar and Hori style of singing.

2. *Gobarhari Bani* was invented by Ata Hussen Khan (the name of Tansen). It admitted Khayal Asthai and Tarana style of singing.

3. *Dagur Bani* was invented by Suraj Khan. It admitted Kaul Kalbana style.

4. *Nahar Bani* was invented by Chand Khan. It treated Folk music.

12 Banis of Kawali methods were attributed to the Genius Amir Khusaro viz. Naksha-gul, Roza, Guzzal, Koul, Kalbana, Soz, Sufi, Nigar, Tanatill, Baeellat and Sohla.

After the Muslim period these Banis were replaced by gharanas as given below :—

1. *Gwalior Gharana :*—Rahmat Khan (death 1922)
   Balkrishna Buva (1886—1950)

Ram Krishna Buva Vajhe, Nisar Hussen, Raja Bhaiya Poochhwale.

2. *Agra Gharana* :— Natthan Khan (1840—1900)
   Faiyaz Khan (1886—1950)

Abdulla Khan, Jagannath Buwa.

3. *Jaipur Gharana* :— Alladiya Khan (1855—1945)
   Bhaskar Buwa Bakhale (1869—1922)
   (Gwalior, Agra and Jaipur)

Haidar Khan, Mogo Bai Pundarikar, Manjee Khan, Kesar Bai, Bhurjee Khan, Malik Arjun Mansoor, Karamat Ali Khan.

4. *Kirana Gharana* :— Abdul Karim Khan (1872—1937)
   Wahid Khan (death 1949).

Hira Bai Barodkar, Ram Babu Sawai Gandharva, Bhim Sen Joshi, Suresh Babu Mane Ganpat Buwa Behre.

Besides these Gharanas some musicians had started their own schools such as :—

1. Mustaq Hussen Khan Rampur

2. Nazeer Khan Bhindi Bazar

3. Aman Ali Khan Bhindi Bazar

4. Anjani Bai Malpekar Bhindi Bazar

5. Bare Gulam Ali Khan Paliyala

6. Amir Khan Indore

7. Narain Rao Bal Gandharva

8. Master Krishna Rao

9. Kumar Gandharva

The System of Education in Old Time

The system of education in those days was different from what we see today. Most of the educational instructions imparted education face to face. Practical education was more than mere theory imparted through lecturers, and notation system of the songs. The degrees awarded at the time of Rag Ragini system were as follows :—

1.   (Vaggayekar)
2.   (Nayuk)
3.   (Pandit)
4.   (Gandharva)
5.   (Kalawant)
6.   (Guni)
7.   (Kavval)

1. *Vaggayekar*—The musician who possessed the knowledge of poetic and musical notation system, i.e. one who had the knowledge of composing poems and singing them through proper notation was called the Vaggayekar. A musician should possess the perfect knowledge of music alongwith sound knowledge of language, producing the song in sweet musical rhythm, so that he may attract the audience towards his song.

2. *Nayuk*—The degree of Nayuk was held the most gracious degree in old Indian Music. This degree was awarded to the musician who, after receiving education under the well-versed master of subject and should have possessed the knowledge of recognising, displaying and teaching every type of classical Raga in a melodious and enchanting way through his sweet voice with the intricate and varied technicalities. He should have perfect knowledge of Goyakies of old teachers and also should possess the knowledge of tuning these Ragas.

In old Indian Music literature, we read the names of 30 Nayuks. Out of these thirty, nineteen were of old Mata's time like Shameshwar, Bharat, Kalinath and Lord Krishna etc. Seven of them like Gopal Nayuk, Baijoo Bavara, Amir Khusro, Dhannu, Maksu, Pandavo and Lohan have been in times of Allauddin Khilzee. Urju, Bhagwan, Jasode and Dalow have been mentioned after times of Khilzee.

3. *Pandit*—One who possessed the perfect knowledge of music theory alongwith practical general knowledge of singing was called the 'Pandit'

This term literally signified a Doctor of Music and was applied to those who professed to teach the theory of music and did not engage in its practice.

4. *Gandharva*—A musician who possessed the knowledge of singing and playing Margi and Deshi only was called the Gandharva.

5. *Kalavanta*—Kalavant Musician was one who possessed the practical and theoretical knowledge of vocal and instumental music. According to some thinkers Dhrupad musician is also the Kalavant.

6. *Guni*—The musician having knowledge of modern Ragas and to sing and play them was called the Guni.

7. *Kavval*—The musician having command over Khyal, Kaul Kalbana and Naksha was called Kavval.

English Period

In the first half of 18th century, Pt. Sriniwas wrote Raga Vibodha. He like Ahobal established 12 shuddha and Vikrit swaras on different lengths of string. He made his own shuddha Thata equal to the Kafee Thata of today. He was the last author of medieval India. In south India, Raja Tula Ji Rao Bhonsale took an interest in raising the standard of music. He wrote Sangeet Sangeetamritam to describe the system of music in South India.

After the downfal of the Mughal Empire in India the Europeans started to rule over the country but the Indian music found no impetous from them because they did not appreciate the Indian musical system with the result that the educated society of the country started to hate it. Even then, some English musicians like William Johns, Sir W. Austley, Captain Day and Captain Willard etc. studied the characteristics of Indian music. Maharaja Pratap Singh (1779—1804) of Jaipur organised a conference and invited the talented musicians of the country to attend it. After the conference he wrote Sangeetsara (Epitome of Music) and took Bilawal Thata as Shuddha Thata. Then in 1842 Krishna Nand Bias wrote Sangeet Kalpadrum in which he wrote some songs without notations. In 1813 Mahammad Raza of Patna wrote Nagmate-Asafi on music. He supposed Bilawal Thata and categorised Ragas on thata system and condemned old Rag-Ragini System. The definitions of Ragas are still appreciated in India.

In the meanwhile Tanjore became the centre of musical activities in South India. The famous musicians of South India at that time were Tiyag Raja, Shyam, Shastri and S. Dikshidhan. In Bengal, Raja S.M. Tagore and other musicians considered Rag-Ragini system correct and wrote books on the same outlines.

In 19th century some Urdu writers wrote some books on music in Urdu language Some of the well known books where Sharma-e-ishrat by Sadaq Ali Khan, in 1874, Nagma Sitar by Mirza Rahim Beg Khan in 1891. Nad Vinod Granth by Gusain Pannalal Chunnilal in 1895 and Quanoon Raga and composition of classical songs. In all these books Bilawal Thata has been supposed as the Shuddha Thata.

In the last decades of the 19th century there was a revolutionary change in the field of music due to two grand personalities. One of them was Pandit Vishnu Digamber Paluskar and the other was Pt. Vishnu Narain Bhatkande.

Pt. Vishnu Digamber Paluskar was born on 18th August, 1872 in small estate called Kurundwad in Maharashtra. He received the training of music from Sri Bal Krishana Buva for about 9 years. After the study he made up his mind to work for the uplift of music and respect of musicians in the society. He proved himself a talented musician in a very short time. He could have lead a luxurious life as a court musician but he devoted his whole life for the betterment of music. He laid foundation of the Gandharava Maha Vidyalaya in Lahore in 1901 for the musical education of boys and girls. He postulated his own system of notation. He also started tutorial classes to make well versed music teachers by providing free board and lodge. There are about 300 branches of Gandharva Mahavidyalaya all over India with its own system of notation.

25

Paluskar made tours all over India. He always tried to maintain respect of musicians and performers of the programme. In 1916, All India Music Conference was held in Baroda with the efforts of Sri Vishnu Narain Bhatkhande. He read his articles on notation. In 1918 the first musical conference was held in Gandharva Mahavidyalaya under the Presidentship of Sri M. R. Jayakar. In 1923 he sang Vande Matram song to a spell bound audience. In 1930 he organised Sangeet Sabhas to support Avagya Andolan of M.K. Gandhi. He was really a rishi in the true sense and was a perfect Nayuk and Vacyakar in true sense. Towards the end of his life he left all the work to be finished by his followers and devoted he rest of his life in devotion to God.

Pt. Vishnu Narain Bhatkhande was born on 10th of August, 1860 at Balkeshwar in Gujarat State. He graduated himself in 1883 and after that passed Law in 1890. He was very much eager to learn music hence started his historical tour in 1904 and found out many things new. He attended many music meetings and heard music from musicians of that time. He felt that their song did not have proper notation system. Hence he heard their music and drew out of his own notations system and wrote a series Karamik Book in 6 parts of the collections he made and also wrote Hindustani Sangeet Paddhati in Marathi language in four parts on music theory. In Sanskrit language he wrote two books Lakshya Sangeet and Abhinava Rag Manjari. In these two books he threw some light on old Indian music to remove the prevailing doubts in it. He made Bilawal Thata as his foundation scale. The new system he started after consultation of various books available upto that time is clearly depicted in his two other books in English language (1) A comparative study of some of leading the music systems in 15th, 16th, 17th and 18th centuries. (2) A Short History of Survey of the Music of upper India.

For the popularity of Indian music he organised conferences at many places such as Baroda, Delhi, Lucknow and Varanasi etc. and established colleges at Baroda, Lucknow and Gwalior by his own efforts. In this way Pt. Vishnu Narain Bhatkhande proved a very successful and appreciable scholar as well as a great reformer and contributor. He was a Pandit of his subject.

In times of Pt. Vishnu Narain Bhatkhande was written Marifulnagmat by Raja Thakur Nawab Ali of Lucknow.

Period of Independent India

After Independence the music gained great popularity. The educated society started to feel necessity of teaching music to their children. It has been now introduced as a special subject in schools and colleges and has become a part of education to the boys and girls from the K.G. classes to the Graduate and Post-Graduate level music is taught as a subject. Besides the educational Institutes, the music conference are also held and various academies are functioning well in various parts of the country. Now-a-days music is getting a charming hold on Film, Television and Radio broadcasting programmes. It is hoped that music in future will achieve more appreciable position in culture and sophisticated families in India and abroad.

4

The Two Systems of Indian Music

After the formation of Sangeet Ratnakar the Indian music was affected by Arab, Greek and Persian elements and blended itself into Hindu Music. The famous musicians of the north migrated to south and kept the old Indian music quite safe. Hence, the Indian music was divided in two systems :

(a)   Northern System or The Hindustani System.

(b)   Southern System or The Karnataki System.

The Northern or the Hindustani System is prevalent in whole of India excepting the Karnataka and Tamil Nadu States where Karnataki system is more popular. The northern system of music is the old Indian system related with the Jati Gayan as the base of musical activities but gradually it was converted into scale system whereas according to southern system of music every type of Raga has been originated out of Thata or Scales called Male Raga. The followers of northern system began to popularise new Rag-Raginis and Dhrupad Gayakies by making Rag-Ragini system as their base.

After 18th Century AD the northern system brought about a new change and Mohammad Raza accepted the Scales as the originator of Ragas supposing Bilaval Thata as a natural scale. He opposed the Rag-Ragini system on several points. After some time the northern system also ran under a new change with some modifications by Vishnu Narain Bhat Khande. Pt. Vishnu Narain Bhatkhande laid foundation of a system of music which became popular in about whole of India but he admits that both the systems principally differ from one another. But if both the systems are studied closely they would represent close similarities with one another and further if we take the climate language, religion and standard of living into consideration, we would come to the conclusion that the basic dissimilarities are negligible. Now the necessity is that the talented musicians should make united effort to bring both of the systems under one and the difference of both the systems should be minimised by the mutual understanding of studying the basic principles of each of them. If we study both the systems in some greater details we would come to know that the difference now lies

27

in manner and style of displaying, formation of Talas and the names of Ragas. Rest of the things are nearly the same both in northern and southern systems of music.

The musical representation in films does not make any difference of northern and southern style. The music of filmstars had eradicated the territorial diversities of music. It has brought north and south together. The modern music draws no line of demarcation between northern and southern styles. If the same is also done by the musicians of stage, then the music as a whole will have greater scope and solidarity and further a more influencial and natural musical environment can be created before the musical circle of the world. Now I would like to bring the basic difference into the notice of the eager musicians :—

The comparison of Northern and Southern Systems of music :

1. Both the systems follow the origin of Swaras from Shrutis and Shrutis from Nada.
2. Both systems admit the 22 Shrutis and form their natural and distorted notes on them.
3. In both the systems only twelve natural and distorted notes have been considered.
4. In both of the systems the division of Shrutis among notes is as follows :—
   Sa Ma Pa four each
   Re and Dha three each
   Ga and Nee two each.
5. Both of the northern and southern musicians admit Thata System.
6. Both the systems agree on the point that the 72 Thatas have borne out of their natural and distorted notes as is supported by Pandit Vyankat Mukhee also.
7. In both the systems only Ragas are played and sung and improvisation and the Tanas are used in both the systems.
8. According to both the systems the Ragas of less than 5 notes are declared unpopular.
9. Both systems show the co-relation of Talas with songs,
10. Both systems support the time factor in music.

Dissimilarities

The position of notes differ in both the systems. According to southern system the fixation of Sa note is on fourth Shruti while according to northern system the Sa note is fixed on first shruti.

Now-a-days the movement of Shrutis is not visible in both the systems. Both the systems favour the same position of notes because the notes, which are fixed on the length of string, show that fixation of notes on Shrutis is the same. We are giving below the position of notes, length of string and the number of vibrations :—

Shuddha and Vikrit Swaras (Swar Mel Kala Nidhi)

Number of shrutis	Shuddha swaras	Vikrit-Swaras		Ramamatya's special nomenclature
		Sharangdev	Ramamatya	
1		Kaisiki Nee	Kaisiki Nee	Shatshruti Dha
2		Kakali Nee	Kakli Nee	
3		Chyutha Sa	Chyutha Sa	Chyuthashadaja Nee
4	Sa	Achyutha Sa		
5				
6				
7	Re	Vikrit Re		
8				
9	Ga			Panchashruti Re
10		Shadharana Ga	Shadharana Ga	Shatshruti Re
11		Antara Ga	Antara Ga	
12		Chyutha Ma	Chyutha Ma	Chuthamadhyama Ga
13	Ma	Achyutha Ma		
14				
15		Vikrit Pa	Chyutha Pa	Chuthapancham Ma
16		Kaisiki Pa		
17	Pa			
18				
19				
20	Dha	Vikrit Dha		
21				
22	Nee			Panchshruti Dha

As shown above Sharangdev has accepted 7 Shuddha and 12 Vikrit Swaras making total of 19 whereas later on Ramamatya 7 Shuddha and 7 Vikrit and 7 Special thus totalling 21 Notes. These Swaras continued in Southern System for a long time.

Notes of Northern and Southern Systems

S. No.	Southern System	Shruti		Northern System
1	Kaishiki Nee	1	Tivra	Sa Natural
		2	Kumud Vati	
2	Kaklee Nee	3	Manda	Re Half Tone
3	Natural Sa	4	Chhando Vati	
		5	Daya Vati	Re Natural
		6	Ranjani	
4	Natural Re	7	Raktika	Ga Half Tone
		8	Raudri	Ga Natural
5	Natural Ga	9	Krodhi	
6	Simple Ga	10	Vajrika	Ma Natural
		11	Prasarini	—
7	Antara Ga	12	Preeti	M' Sharp
8	Natural Ma	13	Marjani	
		14	Kshiti	Pa Natural
		15	Rakta	
9	Varali Ma	16	Sandeepini	Dha Half Tone
10	Natural Pa	17	Alapini	
		18	Mandanti	Dha Natural
		19	Rohini	
11	Natural Dha	20	Ramya	Nee Half Tone
		21	Urga	
12	Natural Nee	22	Kshobhini	Nee Natural

Now-a-days both Northern and Southern Systems admit theory of seven Shuddha and 6 Vikrit Swaras of 12 total Notes in an Octave.

Statement of Length of String according to Vibration

Notes	Length of string	Vibrations
Sa	36″	240
Re	32″	270
Ga	30″	288
Ma	27″	320
Pa	24″	360
Dha	21½″	405
Nee	20″	432
Sa	18″	480

Swaras of Manjari Kar

Notes	Length of string	Vibrations
Sa	36″	240
Re	32″	270
Ga	28-2/3″	310-17/43
Ma	27″	320
Pa	24″	360
Dha	21-1/3″	405
Nee	19-1/9″	452-4/43

In both types of above notes the interval between Sa and Re is equal. The difference is only in Gandhar and Nishad. If we study the interval between Sa and Re on the basis of Shrutis, we see the interval of one Shruti. Only because the Shruti difference between Sa and Re according to Southern System is three while according to Northern System it is four, hence in Northern System Sa is fixed on first Shruti and Re on fifth while in Southern System Sa is fixed on fourth Shruti and Re on seventh. The same interval is seen between Pa and Dha but if we fix the notes on the basis of length of string, then the difference is not seen. This shows shrutis are of no use after fixing the notes on the length of string and in both ways the notes seem to be the same. The positions of Ga and Nee of half tone note in Northern System. Now the difference is only of supposing notes. Ga and Nee are the natural notes in Southern System but they do not show any difference at the time of singing :

1. In Southern System the position of Tali is on the first Matra of every division.

2. At the time of showing Talas by sign of Matra every Tala is shown as given in the Tal-chapter.

3. In this system there is no place of Khali. There is only dot for it.

4. In this system the two mediums are not used at a time.

5. Talas and Matras are of greater prominence in this system.

Details of 18 Jatis Sung in Old Time

S. No.	Category	Ansha	Niyasa	Apniyasa	Murchhana	Shadava omitted notes	Odava omitted notes
1	Shadaji	SGMPD	S	GP	Uttarayato	N	O
2	Arshabhi	RDN	R	RDN	Shuddha Shadaj	S	SP
3	Gandhari	SGMPN	G	SP	Pauravi	R	RD
4	Madhyama	SRMPD	M	SRMPD	Kalopanata	G	GN
5	Panchami	RP	P	RPN	Kalopanata	G	GN
6	Dhaivati	RD	D	RDM	Abhimarudata	P	SP
7	Nishadi	NRG	N	NRG	Ashvakanta	P	SP
8	Shadaj Kaushiki	SGP	G	SPN	—	O	O
9	Shadajo Deechyava	SMDN	M	SD	Ashvakanta	R	RP
10	Shadaj Madhyama	SRGMPDN	SM	SRGMPDN	Matsarikrit	N	GN
11	Gandharo Deechyava	SM	M	SD	Pauravi	R	O
12	Rakto Gandhari	SGMPN	G	M	Kalopanata	R	RD
13	Kaishiki	SGMPDN	GPN	SGMPDN	Harinashva	R	RD
14	Madhya modi-chyava	P	M	SD	Sauveeree	O	O
15	Karmaravi	RPDN	P	RPDN	Suddha Madhya	O	O
16	Gandhar Panchami	P	G	RP	Harinashva	O	O
17	Andhari	RGPN	G	RGPN	Sauvery	S	O
18	Nandayanti	P	G	MP	Hirasyaka	S	O

Ramamatya's 20 Melas, interpreted in terms of the Modern Melas

N.B.—In this figure three points should be remembered :—

1. Antara Ga and Chyuthamadhyama Ga should be deemed to be practically identical; and so also, in the case of Kakali Nee and Chyuthashadja Nee.

2. Panchasruti Re and Dha should be deemed to be the modern Chathusruti Re and Dha.

3. Venkatamukhi's Sudha and Shatsruti Swaras should be deemed to be the same as Ramamatya's.

S. No.	Ramamatya's Twenty Melas	Modern Melas	
		Carnatic	Hindustani
1	Mukhari	Kanakangi	
2	Malavagowla	Mayamalavagowla	Bhairava
3	Sriraga	Kharaharapriya	Kafi
4	Saranganata	Sankarabharana	Bilaval
5	Hindola	Natabhairavi	Asaveri
6	Sudharamakriya	Kamavardhani	Poorvi
7	Desakshi	Soolini	
8	Kannadagowla	Vagadisvari	
9	Sudhanata	Chalanata	
10	Ahiri	Girvani	
11	Nadaramakriya	Dhenuka	
12	Sudhavarali	Jalavarali	
13	Rithigowla	Vanaspathi	
14	Vasanthabhairavi	Vakulabharana	
15	Kedaragowla	Sankarabharana	
16	Hejujji	Mayamalavagowla	
17	Samavarali	Ganamurthi	
18	Revagupthi	Gayakapriya	
19	Samantha	Chalanata	
20	Kambhoji	Sankarabharana	

Ramamatya's Janak-Janya Ragas

S. No.	Melas (20)	Janya Ragas (64)
1	Mukhari	Mukhari and a few Gram Ragas
2	Malavagowla	(1) Malavagowla, (2) Lalitha, (3) Bowli, (4) Sourashtra (5) Gurjari, (6) Mechabowli, (7) Palamanjari. (8) Gunda Kariya, (9) Sindhuramakariya, (10) Chayagowla (11) Karanji, (12) Mangalakowsika, (13) Kannadabangla (14) Malhari etc.
3	Sri Raga	(1) Sri Raga, (2) Bhairavi, (3) Gowli, (4) Dhaniyasi (5) Sudhabhairavi, (6) Velavali, (7) Malavasari, (8 Sankarabhavana, (9) Andoli, (10) Devagandhari (11) Madhyomadi etc.
4	Saranganata	(1) Sarangrata, (2) Saveri, (3) Salangabhairavi, (4) Nat narayani, (5) Sudhavasanta, (6) Purvagola, (7) Kunthala Varali, (8) Bhinna Shadja, (9) Narayani etc.
5	Hindol	(1) Hindol, (2) Marga Hindol, (3) Bhupala
6	Sudharamkriya	(1) Sudharamkriya, (2) Padi, (3) Arda Deshi, (4) Dipak
7	Deshakshi	Deshakshi
8	Kannadagowla	(1) Kannadagowla, (2) Ghantarava, (3) Sudhabangala, (4) Chayanta, (5) Turuska Todi, (6) Nagadhavani, (7) Devakriya
9	Sudhanta	Sudhanata etc.
10	Ahiri	Ahiri etc.
11	Nada Ramkriya	Nada Ramkriya etc.
12	Shuddha Varali	Shuddha Varali etc.
13	Rithigowla	Rithigowla etc.
14	Vasant Bhairavi	(1) Vasanthabhairavi, (2) Somaraga etc.
15	Kedaragowla	(1) Kedaragowla, (2) Narayangowla etc.
16	Hejujji	Hejujji and few Gram Ragas
17	Samavarali	Samavarali Do
18	Revagupthi	Revagupthi Do
19	Samantha	Samantha etc.
20	Kambhoji	Kambhoji etc.

Characteristics of a Few Ramamatyas Derivative Ragas

S.No.	Ragas	Melas	Graha	Amsa	Niyasa	Time of Singing	Rank	Reasons for Rank	Remarks
1	Lalitha	Malavagowla	Sa	Sa	Sa	First watch of the day	S. Sh.	Pa omitted	
2	Bowli	-do-	Ma	Ma	Ma	First half of the day	S. Sh.	Pa omitted	Ma omitted in another version
3	Gurjari	-do-	Re	Re	Re	First watch of the day	S. Sh.	Pa omitted though retained in descent	
4	Gundakriya	-do-	Sa	Sa	Sa	Former part of the day	M.Sh.	Dha omitted though retained at times	
5	Kannada Bangla	-do-	Ga	Ga	Ga	Morning	M. Sh.	Re omitted	
6	Malhari	-do-	Dha	Dha	Dha	Day break	S. O.	Ga and Nee omitted	
7	Saurasthra	-do-	Sa	Sa	Sa	Evening	I. S.	...	
8	Bhairavi	Sri Raga	Sa	Sa	Sa	Latter part of the day	S. S.	...	
9	Dhanyasi	-do-	Sa	Sa	Sa	Morning	S. O.	Re and Dha omitted	
10	Velavali	-do-	Dha	Dha	Dha	Day break	M. S.	Re and Pa omitted in descent	
11	Sankara-Bharana	-do-	Sa	Sa	Sa	...	I. S.	...	Resembles Samantha
12	Andoli	-do-	Pa	Pa	Pa		I. O.	Ga and Nee omitted	
13	Madhyamadi	-do-	Ma	Ma	Ma	Latter part of the day	M. O.	Re and Dha omitted	
14	Malavasri	-do-	Sa	Sa	...	Always	S. Sh.	Ga and Nee omitted	
15	Sovery	Saranganata	Dha	Dha	Dha	Day break	I. O.	Ga and Nee omitted	
16	Sudha Vasantha	-do-	Sa	Sa	Sa	Fourth part of the day	S. Sh.	Pa omitted though retained in descent	
17	Bhina Shadaja	-do-	Sa	...	Sa	Always	I. Sh.	Ma omitted	
18	Narayani	-do-	Ga	Ga	Ga	Morning	M.S.	Re omitted in descent	
19	Bhupal	Hindol	Sa	Sa	Sa	Always	I. Sh.	M and Nee omitted	
20	Ghantarava	Kannada gowla	Dha	Dha	Dha	Always	I. S.	Ga omitted	
21	Nagadhvani	-do-	Sa	Sa	Sa	Always	I.S.	Sounds with Ma nicely in Mandra	
22	Som Raga	Vasant Bhairvi	Sa	Sa	Sa	Always	I. S.	...	
23	Padi	Shuddha Ramkriya	Sa	Sa	Sa	Fourth part of the day	M. Sh.	Ga omitted	

Thatas of Southern System

S. No.	Thatas of Southern System	Notes of Thatas						
1	Mukhari	Sa	Re	Re	Ma	Dha	Dha	Ṡa
2	Revagupthi	S	R	G	M	P	D	D	Ṡ
3	Samvarali	S	R	R	M	P	D	N	Ṡ
4	Todi	S	R	G	M	P	D	N	Ṡ
5	Nad Ramsri	S	R	G	M	P	D	N	Ṡ
6	Bhairava	S	R	G	M	P	D	N	Ṡ
7	Basant	S	R	G	M	P	D	N	Ṡ
8	Basant Bhairavi	S	R	G	M	P	D	N	Ṡ
9	Malva Gaud	S	R	G	M	P	D	N	Ṡ
10	Reeli Gaud	S	R	G	M	P	D	N	Ṡ
11	Abhir Nata	S	R	G	M	P	D	N	Ṡ
12	Hameer	S	R	G	M	P	D	N	Ṡ
13	Shuddha Ramshri	S	R	G	M	P	D	N	Ṡ
14	Shuddha Varati	S	R	G	Ḿ	P	D	N	Ṡ
15	Sri	S	R	G	M	P	D	N	Ṡ
16	Kalyan	S	R	G	Ḿ	P	D	N	Ṡ
17	Kambodi	S	R	G	M	P	D	N	Ṡ
18	Malari	S	R	G	Ḿ	P	D	N	Ṡ
19	Samant	S	G	G	Ḿ	P	D	N	Ṡ
20	Karne Gaud	S	G	M	M	P	D	N	Ṡ
21	Deshakshi	S	G	G	M	P	D	N	Ṡ
22	Shuddha Nata	S	G	G	M	P	D	N	Ṡ
23	Sarang	S	R	Ḿ	P	P	N	N	Ṡ

5

Tal System of Old Time

The following 7 Talas had been adopted in Indian music in old time.

1. Ek Tal	2. Roopak Tal
3. Jhap Tal	4. Triput Tal
5. Math Tal	6. Dhruva Tal
7. Ath Tal	

Each of the above Tala has been expressed in 5 Jatis (Categories). It means the number of Talas popular at that time consisted $7 \times 5 = 35$. The 5 Jatis were as follows :—

1. Chatsar Jati

2. Tisar Jati

3. Khand Jati

4. Misrit Jati

5. Sankeern Jati

The value of the Matras changes with the change of Matras of Laghu. But khands remain the same. The Laghu Matras are as follows :—

1.	Chatsar Jati	4 Matras
2.	Tisar Jati	3 Matras
3.	Khand Jati	5 Matras
4.	Misrit Jati	7 Matras
5.	Sankeern Jati	9 Matras

The system of finding out the time of these matras was as follows :—

8 Kshan	=1 Lava		2 Anudrut	=1 Drut
8 Lavas	=1 Kasta		2 Drut	=1 Laghu
8 Kastas	=1 Nimish		2 Laghu	=1 Guru
8 Nimish	=1 Kala		3 Laghu	=1 Pulat
4 Kalas	=1 Anudrut		4 Laghu	=1 Kak pad

37

Time of Kshana

1	Matra is called 1 Bram Anudrut		
2	Matras	=Drut	=2
3	,,	=Drut Bram	=2+1
4	,,	=Laghu	=4
5	,,	=Laghu Bram	=4+1
6	,,	=Laghu Drut	=4+2
7	,,	=Laghu Drut Bram	=4+2+1
8	,,	=Guru	=8
9	,,	=Guru Bram	=8+1
10	,,	=Guru Drut	=8+2
11	,,	=Guru Drut Bram	=8+2+1
12	,,	=Pulat	=12
13	,,	=Pulat Bram	=12+1
14	,,	=Pulat Drut	=12+2
15	,,	=Pulat Drut Bram	=12+2+1
16	,,	=Kak Pat	=16

Hundreds of Talas can be formed out of above 16 Matras but out of them only 8 or 10 are more popular. The time of Ek Kshan has been calculated as follows :—

If 100 leaves of Lotus (Kamal) taken together pearced with a sharp needle, the time required by the needle to pass through one leaf will be called the kshan. This can be calculated even 1/1000 part of a second. This kshan was taken as basic unit to measure time. The four talas which are called Anudrut or Bram are equal to the time of one matra taken as a base of time for one second.

The counting of these Talas was done with a particular sign such as :—

1 Matra (U), 2 Matras (O), 4 Matras (I). For example One Tala having 6 Matras was written as $\frac{|\quad|\quad|\quad|}{o \quad - \quad \times \quad -}$ —Matra of Chatsar Jati=16 i.e. it may increase or decrease but the position of Tali and Khali remains the same as $\frac{|\quad|\quad|\quad|}{o \quad -n \quad \times \quad -}$ — Matras of Chatassar Jati.

Matra (Stroke)—A matra is taken as the shortest time in which a syllable can be properly pronounced. In medium normal speed the time of a matra is presumed to be one second, in fast speed half second and in slow speed two seconds.

Tali—Clapping of hand is called Tali i.e. Theka of Talas having Tali points marked 1,2,3,4 etc.

Khali—Khali means a gap of some matras which bols of Theka play by right hand on tabla only. The left, duggi dhama, remains Khali.

Jati Talas

S. No.	Tal	Jati	Sign	Matras	Name of Talas
1	Ek Tal	Chatassar	1	4	Man Tala
2	,,	Tisar	1	3	Shuddha Tala
3	,,	Khand	1	7	Ram Tala
4	,,	Misra	1	5	Rati Tala
5	,,	Sankeern	1	9	Basu Tala
6	Roopak	Chatassar	10	2+4= 6	Put Tala
7	,,	Tisar	10	2+3= 5	Chakra Tala
8	,,	Misra	10	2+7= 9	Raj Tala
9	,,	Khand	10	2+5= 7	Kul Tala
10	,,	Sankeern	10	2+9=11	Bindu Tala
11	Jhap	Chatassar	IUO	4+1+2= 7	Madhur Tala
12	,,	Tisar	,,	3+1+2= 6	Kadamb Tala
13	,,	Khand	,,	7+1+2=10	Sur Tala
14	,,	Misra	,,	5+1+2= 8	Jan Tala
15	,,	Sankeern	,,	9+1+2=12	Tri Tala
16	Triput	Chatassar	100	4+2+2= 8	Ada Tala
17	,,	Tisar	,,	3+2+2= 7	Shankha Tala
18	,,	Misra	,,	7+2+2=11	Duskar Tala
19	,,	Khand	,,	5+2+2= 9	Bhog Tala
20	,,	Sankeern	,,	9+2+2=13	Shukar Tala
21	Mathia	Chatassar	101	4+2+4=10	Sam Tala
22	,,	Tisar	,,	3+2+3= 8	Sar Tala
23	,,	Misra	,,	7+2+7=16	Udai Tala
24	,,	Khand	,,	5+2+5=12	Udirn Tala

S. No.	Tal	Jati	Sign	Matras	Name of Talas
25	Mathia	Sankeern	101	9+2+9=20	Rau Tala
26	Dhruva	Chatassar	1011	4+2+4+4=14	Shree Tala
27	,,	Tisar	,,	3+2+3+3=11	Mantree Tala
28	,,	Misra	,,	7+2+7+7=23	Purna Tala
29	,,	Khand	,,	5+2+5+5=17	Praman Tala
30	,,	Sankeern	,,	9+2+9+9=29	Bhuvan Tala
31	Ath	Chatassar	1100	4+4+2+2=12	Lekh Tala
32	,,	Tisar	,,	3+3+2+2=10	Gupta Tala
33	,,	Misra	,,	7+7+2+2=18	Loop Tala
34	,,	Khand.	,,	5+5+2+2=14	Ved Tala
35	,,	Sankeern	,,	9+9+2+2=22	Dhir Tala

Besides these 35 Talas each one of them has been further divided into 5 rhythmical categories. They are called Panch Gati Bhedas as follows :—

1. Chatasar Gati Bheda $\qquad = 7 \times 5 = 35$
2. Tisar Gati Bheda $\qquad = 7 \times 5 = 35$
3. Khand Gati Bheda $\qquad = 7 \times 5 = 35$
4. Misra Gati Bheda $\qquad = 7 \times 5 = 35$
5. Sankeerna Gati Bheda $\qquad = 7 \times 5 = 35$

$$35 \times 5 = 175$$

6

Nada (Sound)

The Sound which is spread all over the creation of God is called the 'Brahmma Nada'. Brahmma Nada is the medium of all human behaviours. Sangeet Ratnakar expresses Nada as follows :

चेतन्यं सर्वभूतानां विवृत्तं जगदात्मना ।
नादन्ब्रह्म तदानन्दम् द्वितीय मुपास्महे ॥

—(संगीत रत्नाकर)

Nada exists in every living being. Hence, it is called the Brahmma Nada.

नादेन व्यज्यते वर्णः पदं वर्णात् पदाद्वचः ।
बचसो व्यवहारोऽयं नादाधीनमतो जगत ॥

—(संगीत दर्पण)

The alphabets are pronounced with the help of Nada. These alphabets make words, sentences and language. In this way Nada is the supreme power over all human activities.

Nada is of two kinds :—

1. Ahat Nada
2. Anahat Nada.

आहतोऽनाहृत श्चेति द्विधा नादो निगद्यते ।
सोऽयं प्रकाशते पिण्डे तस्मात् पिण्डोऽभिधीयते ॥

—(संगीत दर्पण)

Ahat Nada.—This Nada has originated from human body.

आत्मना प्रेरितं चित्तं बहिमांहति देहजम् ।
बृह्मग्रन्थि स्थितं प्राणं स प्रेरयति पावकः ॥
पावक-प्रेरितः श्रोऽय क्रमादूर्ध्वं पथे चरन ।
अति सूक्ष्म ध्वनि नांमो हृदि सूक्ष्म गले पुनः ॥
पुष्ठं शीर्खेतव पुष्ठं च कृत्रिम बदने तथा ।
अविभविय तील्येवं प्रश्चधा कील्यते बुधैः ॥

—(संगीत दर्पण)

41

The mind is guided by the soul which increases bodily heat and that heat moves the air of body upward. The amount of air increases from umbilical chord to the head. It vibrates very lightly in the umbilical chord, light in heart, sufficient in throat. When it comes to the mouth, it is reshaped.

Ahat Nada:—When air and heat of body strike together they produce sound. In simple form we can represent it as the sound produced by striking of two bodies together.

न कारं प्रांणनामनं दकार नमलं विदुः ।
जातः प्राण निग्र संयोगत्तेन नादोऽभि धीयते ॥

—(संगीत दर्पण)

Nada is the sound produced by the combination of bodily heat and air.

Ahat Nada is of two kinds :—

(a) Sound   (b) Word.

Sound :—Sound is produced by the throat directly without any obstruction in the way. It is the natural voice which is produced by the combination of heat of the body and the air.

Word :—Word is the combination of sounds modified by different parts of mouth such as lips, teeth and tongue etc. Some of the sounds are sweet to hear but some are not so. In music we are concerned with the sound which is sweet, amusing and euphonic.

The musical sound can be distinguished in three ways :—
1. By the magnitude of the sound.
2. By the timbre of the sound.
3. By the pitch of the sound.

The magnitude of the sound means the force at which it is coming out of the mouth. It may be light or heavy on the same note.

The timbre of the sound means whether the sound is the characteristic quality of vocal (male-femal or boy and girl), instrumental music or it is produced by some bird or animal. This kind of demarcation is called the timbre of the sound.

The pitch of the sound refers the idea of point from which the sound is produced. It denotes the Octaves—lower, medium or upper.

Besides the above the prolongation of sound also counts much in music. It gives the idea of pause in form of Matras.

Anhat Nada :—

ओइम् अष्टा चक्रा नव द्वारा देवानां पूर्योध्या ।
तस्यां हिरण्ययः कोषः स्वर्गो ज्योतिषावृतः ॥

—(अथर्ववेद काण्ड 10, सूक्त 2, मंत्र 31)

God has gifted the soul with a wonderful body consisting of eight divine nerve centres and circles in all parts and organs and nine portals, that is, two ears, two nostrils, one mouth and two excretary organs. In this mortal body is laid a golden treasure chest of mental tranquiliity, which is full of bliss, begirt with light and wisdom. The Yogis can get emancipation and salvation by understanding these divine circles through Yogic exercises and meditation. There are nine doors or portals of human body.

The Divine Nerve Centres and Circles of Human Body

1. Kundalini-Chakra (कुंडलिनी चक्र) from where Sukshum (सुष्मना) nerve starts.

2. Muladhar Chakra (मूलाधर चक्र) which is in human rectum.

3. Swadhinasthan-Chakra (स्वाधीनाष्ठन चक्र) which lies between Muladhar Chakra and Umbilical Cord.

4. Manipurak Chakra (मणिपूरक चक्र) lies in the centre of Umbilical Cord.

5. Anahat Chakra (अनाहत चक्र) lies in the heart.

6. Vishuddha Chakra (विशुद्ध चक्र) lies in throat.

7. Lalna Chakra (लालना चक्र) lies in tongue.

8. Order Chakra (आज्ञा चक्र) lies between two eye brows.

9. Sahasrar Chakra (सहस्रार चक्र) lies in mind.

The excellent and wonderful construction of human body is surrounded by air and light from all sides. In side this excellent and pleasuresome structure lies the eternal power of God. This power leads us to salvation and emancipation by understanding these divine circles and portals through meditation and exercises.

According to some thinker's the Anahat Nada is out of the power of hearing, hence, it is not included in musical studies, but on the basis of Veda's Mantras, the Anahat Nada is directly related to the heart and every type of ideas which produce different kinds of Tunes and Ragas come out of the heart. When it is expressed in the form of Ragas and Notes it is called the Ahat Nada. It means the Anahat Nada is the root of the origin of music. This Anahat Nada is very essential for Indian music for Rag Alapas. It is the source of building music. The Nada which has been described in the above sloka, is called the Anahad Nada. They can be enjoyed by the Yogis only at the time of Samadhi. This Anhad Nada is neither heard through ears nor has any body interpreted it. Just as a deaf person is helpless to express the sweetness of a sound, so also the Yogis are unable to express the truth of this Nada. Now it is proved that Anahat and Anhad nadas are two different things. Anahat Nada obtained by destroying the Anahat Circle as mentioned above.

7

Shrutis (Sympathetic Notes)

Shruti—Shruti is a Sanskrit word which means to hear or heard. It is originated from Nada. The music literature describes 22 shrutis.

The word shrutis has been defined as the small sounds which can easily be heard by the ears and can clearly be recognized. They are very minutely demarcated from one another. They are a kind of swaras. The shrutis which are clearly pronounced by giving greater pauses, take the shape of swaras. Shrutis are distinguished from swaras on the basis of pause which is comparatively greater between swaras than shrutis. Sangeet Parijat explains shrutis as follows :

श्रुतियाः स्युः स्वराभिवाः श्रावण त्वेन हैतुना ।

अहि कुण्डल वत्तव्व वेदोक्ति शास्त्र सम्मता ॥

—(संगीत पारिजात)

The sound which can be heard is called the shruti. Shruti is not different from swaras. They are very closely connected just as a snake with the ring around its body.

सर्वश्चि श्रुतयस्तत्त द्रागेषु स्वरतां गताः । ।

रागाः हेतुत्व एतापां श्रुति संज्ञैव सम्मता ॥

All the shrutis are converted into Swaras in Raga *i.e.* the shruti on which we pronounce a sound, is converted into swara at that time.

The experts of music have made the shrutis on the basis of the nerves of the body *i.e.* the nerves which originate nada also produce 22 shrutis.

हृद्‌ध्वं नाडिकारथ द्राविश व्यणुति राजनाडीषु ।

तावन्तः श्रुति सज्ञा स्युर्नादा पर परोच्योच्या ॥

—(राग विबोध)

The nerves which lie in heart are covered by *Ida*, *Pingla and* Shushumna. There are 22 crooked (oblique) and hollows tiny nerves connected with them and from these

22 nerves come out 22 shrutis with the stroke (pressure) of air. These shrutis go on developing gradually one after the other.

Sitar is the most appropriate instrument to understand shrutis. If at the interval of strings of "Sa" and "Re" on Sitar, are joined 3 more frets and the sound is produced with the stroke of mizrab, these fine sounds produced between "Sa" and "Re" will be the shrutis. The second method of establishing shrutis on sitar is divide the interval between the "Sa" of medium Octave and the "Sa" of upper Octave in 22 equal parts and join 22 frets. Now the interval between each fret will be equal to one shruti. For example :

If we strike the mizrab on the string of about 36″ or 90 cms. of the Sitar, it will produce the first Shruti or "Sa" of medium Octave and the sound which will come out at about 18″ or 45 cms. will be the "Sa" of upper Octave or the first Shruti, and if we join 22 frets in the length 18″ or 45 cms. string, then the shruti is a complete unit divided in equal intervals. The interval between the frets will be equal to 25/11 cms. or one shruti. The 2 types of shrutis which are confirmed by the musical literature are given below :

Chart of 22 Shrutis

Shruti	Swara	Narada's Names	Sharngadev's Names	Swara
1.		Sidha	Theevra	
2.		Prabhavathi	Kumudvati	
3.		Kantha	Manda	
4.	Sa	Suprabha	Chandovati	Sa
5.		Sika	Dayavati	
6.		Dipthimati	Ranjani	
7.	Re	Ugra	Ratika	Re
8.		Hladi	Rowdri	
9.	Ga	Nirviri	Krodhi	Ga
10.		Dira	Vajrika	
11.		Sarpasaha	Prasarini	
12.		Kshanthi	Preeti	
13.	Ma	Vibhuthi	Marjani	Ma
14.		Malini	Kshiti	
15.		Chapala	Rakta	
16.		Bala	Sandipini	
17.	Pa	Sarvaratna	Alapini	Pa
18.		Shantha	Madanti	
19.		Vikalini	Rohini	
20.	Dha	Hridayonmalini	Ramya	Dha
21.		Visarini	Ugra	
22.	Nee	Prasuna	Kshobini	Nee

Nature of Shruti

Shruti No.	Name of Shruti	Nature of Shruti
1.	Tivra	Deepta
2.	Kumudvati	Ayatah
3.	Mandah	Mridu
4.	Chhandovati	Madhya
5.	Dayavati	Karuna
6.	Ranjani	Madhya
7.	Raktika	Mradu
8.	Raudri	Deepta
9.	Krodhi	Ayata
10.	Vajrika	Deepta
11.	Prasarini	Ayata
12.	Preeti	Mradu
13.	Marjani	Madhya
14.	Kshiti	Mradu
15.	Rakta	Madhya
16.	Sandipini	Ayata
17.	Alapini	Karuna
18.	Mandati	Karuna
19.	Rohini	Ayata
20.	Ramya	Madhya
21.	Ugra	Deepta
22.	Kshobhini	Madhya

8

Swaras (Notes)

In 1813, when Naghmate Asfi was written by Mohammed Raza of Patna, he supposed Bilawal Thata as natural Thata and condemned old Rag-Ragini system. But this system did not become popular.

After this Pt. Vishnu Narain Bhat Khande modified the music system in a new form. He classified Ragas supposing Bilawal Thata as natural Thata and got it confirmed in several musical conferences. In 1926 Maurice College of Hindustani music was started in Lucknow. Through the medium of this college the notes of Bilawal Thata became more and more popular, and got recognition by the Government. I am trying to describe the same in details.
What is Swara

श्रुत्यनतर भावित्वं यस्थानु रणनात्मक:
स्निग्धश्च रंजकश्चसौ स्वर इत्यभिधीयते ।
स्वयंयो राजतेनाद: स स्वर: परिकीर्तित: ॥

The delicate, pleasing, attractive and buzzing sound is called the swara. The swaras have been taken from shrutis and are formed by the combination of several of them.

चतुश्चतुश्च तुश्चैव मध्यम पञ्जमा:
द्वे द्वे निषाद गंधारो त्रिस्मी ऋषभधैवतो ॥

The above sloka explains that Sa, Ma and Pa contain 4 shrutis each, Re and Dha 3 shrutis each while Nee and Ga contain 2 shrutis each respectively.

For example "Sa", "Ma" and "Pa" by the combination of 4 shrutis each "Re" and "Dha" by the combination of 3 shrutis each, and "Ga" and "Nee" by the combination of 2 shrutis each. On account of this fact swaras are comparatively on greater interval than shrutis and can also be distinguished easily.

Shrutis have been divided into 7 swaras as above. To avoid the difficulty of pronouncing them as a whole, only the first letters of the notes have been considered as the

47

representative symbols of the respective notes just as : Sa, Re, Ga, Ma, Pa, Dha and Nee for shadaj, Rishabh, Gandhar, Madhyam, Panchaham, Dhaivat and Nishad respectively.

In vocal and instrumental both types of music, only the Single letter system is mostly used. S, R, G, M, P, D, N.

In Sangeet Parijat the names of Shrutis of Shuddha swaras are given as follows :—

तीव्रा कुमुद्वती मन्दा छन्दोवत्यस्तु पञ्जया: ।
दयावती तुरेजेवि रञ्जनी रक्तितल्यम् ॥
रौद्री क्रोधेति गन्धारे वजिका अथ: प्रसारिणी ।
प्रीतिश्च: मजिनीन्येता श्रुतुयों मध्य माश्रिता: ॥
क्षिति रक्ता च सन्दीपिन्या लापिन्यथा पञ्जभे ।
मन्दनी रोहिणी रम्येत्येतास्चिा स्त्रस्तु धैवते ॥
उग्रा च क्षोभिणीति द्वे निपादे वसत: श्रुनी : ।
इत्यक्ता: सप्तसु प्रोक्ता स्वरेषु श्रुतयो बुधै: ॥

Swaras (Notes)

Full name of the Swara	Symbol	Single letter	English note	No. of Shruti	Name of Shruti
Shadaj	Sa	S	C	4	Tivra, Kumudvati, Manda Chhandovati.
Rishabh	Re	R	D	3	Dayavati, Ranjani, Raktika.
Gandhar	Ga	G	E	2	Raudri Krodhi
Madhyam	Ma	M	F	4	Vajrika, Prasarini, Preeti, Marjani.
Pancham	Pa	P	G	4	Kshiti, Raktika, Sandipini, Alapini.
Dhaivat	Dha	D	A	3	Madanti, Rohini, Ramya,
Nishad	Nee	N	B	2	Ugra, Kshobhini.
7				22	22

The Position of Notes of Old Times

The positions of notes on Shrutis of old times and of modern age differ to a great extent. In old days every note was fixed at the last Shruti such as Sa on 4th Shruti, Re on

7th Shruti, Ga on 9th Shruti, Ma on 13th Shruti, Pa on 17th Shruti, Dha on 20th Shruti and Nee on 22nd Shruti but in modern style the notes are fixed on the first shruti such as :—

Sa on 1st Shruti, Re on 5th Shruti, Ga on 8th Shruti, Ma on 10th Shruti, Pa on 14th Shruti, Dha on 18th Shruti, Nee on 21st Shruti.

The Position of Notes at Shruti Interval of Old and New

Old Swaras	Name of Shrutis		Modern Swaras
Kaushik Nee	1 Teevra		Sa Achal
	2 Kumudvati		
	3 Manda	Re Komal	
Sa	4 Chhandovati		
	5 Dayavati		Re Shuddha
	6 Ranjani		
Re	7 Raktika	Ga Komal	
	8 Raudri		Ga Shuddha
Ga	9 Krodhi		
	10 Vajrika		Ma Shuddha
	11 Prasarini		
	12 Preeti	Ma Tivra	
Ma	13 Marjini		
	14 Kshiti		Pa Achal
	15 Rakta		
	16 Sandipini	Dha Komal	
Pa	17 Alapini		
	18 Madanti		Dha Shuddha
	19 Rohini		
Dha	20 Ramya	Nee Komal	
	21 Ugra		Nee Shuddha
Nee	22 Kshobhini		

Swaras (Notes) Fixed on Shrutis

OLD SYSTEM			NEW SYSTEM		
Swara	Note	Shruti	Swara	Note	Shruti
Sa	C	Chhandovati	Sa	C	Teevra
Re	D	Raktika	Re	D	Dayavati
Ga	E	Krodhi	Ga	E	Raudri
Ma	F	Marjini	Ma	F	Vajrika
Pa	G	Alapihi	Pa	G	Kshiti
Dha	A	Ramya	Dha	A	Madanti
Nee	B	Kshobhini	Nee	B	Ugra

49

The old popular Shuddha Octave resembles with the swaras of Kafee Thata of today and the Shuddha swara octave of modern times is supposed on the basis of Bilaval Thata. Only on the change of position of notes the interval of Shrutis has nearly coincided.

Types of Swaras (Notes)

A. Avikari or Achal (Undistorted Note)

B. Vikari or Chal (Distorted Note)

Avikati Swaras (*Undistorted Note*) :—The notes in which there is no possibility of any sort of change, distortion of form are called the Avikari Swaras (Undistorted Notes). They cannot be converted into half tone or sharp notes. This type of notes are only two Shadaja and Panchama (Sa and Pa) in an Octave. Both of these notes are considered to be achal or fixed. Though in times of Sangeet Ratnakara, Pa note was considered as the distorted note but at this time it is supposed to be undistorted note.

Sa note is the basic note for the other notes as all the seven notes of octave start from Shadaja and it is not prohibited in any of the Raga. Hence this note is supposed to be fixed.

Panchama :— Pa note is undistorted due to two reasons :—

(a) The sound of Panchama is one and a half times higher than note of Shadaja, hence it can harmonize the sound of Shadaja, *i.e.* 'Supreme and helper note, (Vadi and Samvadi Swara).

(b) If the octave is divided into two parts *i.e.* Sa, Re, Ga, Ma and Pa, Dha, Nee Sa, then Sa is supposed to be the originator or starter of the first part Sa, Re, Ga, Ma and Pa of the second part Pa, Dha, Nee, Sa. Hence, this note is supposed as undistorted note like Sa.

On the basis of these two undistorted parts of octave they are called the First and the Second Parts.

Vikrit Swaras (*Distorted Notes*) :—The notes in which there is possibility of distortion in form *i.e.* they can be converted into half tone or sharp notes are called the Vikrit Swaras (Distorted Notes). The distorted notes are five in an Octave *i.e.* Re, Ga, Ma, Dha and Nee. Out of these five Re, Ga, Dha and Nee are in form of Komal Swaras (half tone notes) and Ma is in form of Tivra Swara (sharp note). In this way swaras can be categorised into three types :—

1. Shudha Swara (full tone note)—Sa, Re, Ga, Ma, Pa, Dha, Nee.

2. Komal Swaras (Half tone notes)—Re Ga Dha Nee, these notes will take place

   before the Shudha Swaras (Full tone notes) one or two shrutis downward.

3. Tivra Swara (Sharp note)—Ḿ this note will take place after Ma Shuddha *i.e.* two shrutis upward.

In old times the distorted notes were used in many forms such as simple Ga, Antar Ga, Kaishaki Nee, Kakli Nee and Tivratar Tivratam and Ati Komal Notes etc. But now-a-days only these three types of swaras are popular.

The Shuddha and Vikrit Swaras

S. No.	Note	Single letter	English note	Category	Category
1.	Sa	S	C	Achal	Fixed
2.	Re	R	bD	Komal	Halftone
3.	Re	R	D	Shuddha	Full tone
4.	Ga	G	bE	Komal	Half tone
5.	Ga	G	E	Shuddha	Full tone
6.	Ma	M	F	Shuddha or Komal	Full tone
7.	Ma	M	F	Tivra	Sharp
8.	Pa	P	G	Achal	Fixed
9.	Dha	D	bA	Komal	Half tone
10.	Dha	D	A	Shuddha	Full tone
11.	Nee	N	bB	Komal	Half tone
12.	Nee	N	B	Shuddha	Full tone

The nature, colour and the characteristics of notes have been described in our music literature. It is very essential for the musicians to be conversant with these characteristic features of notes. Without the knowledge of these Swaras, one cannot reach perfection of Ragas.

The notes have the biographical, human and super natural composition as is given in the following statement :

(i) They are human in temperaments.

(ii) They are descended from heavenly bodies.

(iii) The Swaras are produced from various parts of body and trace their lineage from above.

(iv) Some swaras have got temperament.

(v) They are sung in special seasons of the year and hour of the day.

(vi) Sun and Mars are called to be hot. They rule the elements of fire.

(vii) Jupitor and Moon rule water, Venus and Mercury rule air and Saturn rules the earth.

(viii) They are sung at a particular part of the day to produce desired effect at the specific time.

Swara (Note)	Shrutis	God	Colour	Biographical sound	Men age in years	Season
Sa	Teevra, Kumudvati, Manda, Chhandovati	Fire	Pink	Peacock	70	Cold and moist
Re	Davayati, Ranjani, Raktika	Brahmma	Green	Papiya	60	Cold dry
Ga	Raudri, Krodhi	Sarasvati	Orange	Goat	50	Cold and mois
Ma	Vajrika, Prasarini, Preeti, Marjini	Mahadeo	Purple	Crane	40	Hot and dry
Pa	Kshiti, Raktika, Sandeepini, Alapini	Lakshmi	Red	Coel and Cucoo	30	—
Dha	Madanti, Rohini, Ramya	Ganesh	Yellow	Snake	20	Hot and cold
Nee	Ugra, Kishobhini	Sun	Black	Elephant	10	Cold dry

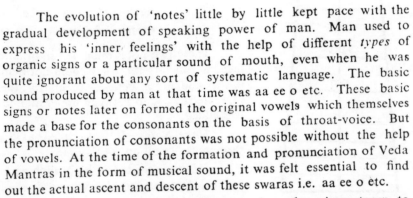

Evolution of 'Notes'

The evolution of 'notes' little by little kept pace with the gradual development of speaking power of man. Man used to express his 'inner feelings' with the help of different *types* of organic signs or a particular sound of mouth, even when he was quite ignorant about any sort of systematic language. The basic sound produced by man at that time was aa ee o etc. These basic signs or notes later on formed the original vowels which themselves made a base for the consonants on the basis of throat-voice. But the pronunciation of consonants was not possible without the help of vowels. At the time of the formation and pronunciation of Veda Mantras in the form of musical sound, it was felt essential to find out the actual ascent and descent of these swaras i.e. aa ee o etc.

The formation of notes had to pass through various stages to achieve the present shape.

One Note—First of all one note came into existence for musical expressions as we find in many Vedic Granthas.

This note took two shapes :—

(a) Tan Swara

(b) Pravachan Swara.

I. *Tan Swara*—Tan means the prolongation of sound. It was used at the time of Pranayam. At the time of Pranayam when one throws out air he pronounces Om......m spontaneously. This note contained one shruti.

In many of the Vedic granthas we find :—

तानोऽन्येषां ब्राह्मण स्वर: ॥ 3 । 27 ॥

तान एवाङ्गो पांङ्गानाम ॥ 3 । 28 ॥

II. *Pravachan Swara*—Pravachan is different from Tan Swara. It means the pronunciation of words in systematic form. It contains 3 Shrutis and does not have much fluctuations in sound. In Vedic granthas the Pravachan Swara has been described as :—

प्रावचन शब्देन ग्रार्प पाठ उच्यते । तत्रभव स्वर: प्रावचन:

———म च त्रैस्वयं लक्षण एव भवति ।

53

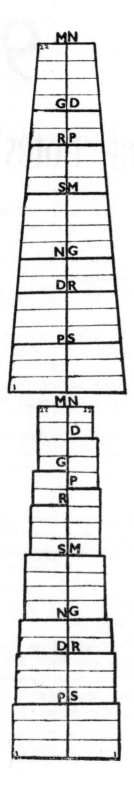

Aarish Patha is pronounced by Pravachan note hence the note performed in Aarish Patha is known as Pravachan Swara. It contains three Shrutis. One note continued to be sung for a long period of time.

Two Notes—After it came two notes which bore their names as Udatta and Anudatta. The features of Udatta & Anudatta are as follows:—

Udatta—Udatta means high pitch sung in upper octave and Anudatta means low pitch sung in lower octave. Ashtadhiyay expresses two notes :—

उदात्त—उच्चैरुदात्त: i.e. sung in high pitch.

अनुदात्त—नीचैरनुदात्त: i.e. sung in low pitch.

These two notes remained in practice for a long period but they faced a difficulty that they could not demarcate the sound between upper and lower octaves to clarify the medium sound. To demarcate the sound between upper and lower octave notes, one note was added.

Three Notes—It was called as Swarit. This addition made three notes in all upto this time.

Udatta is recited in high pitch and is symbolised by a small vertical line marked over the word which is to be pronounced in high pitch as :

अह यशाविनों यंशो विश्वा रूपाःयां वदे

ऋ० खल १ । ७ । १ ॥

Anudatta is recited in low pitch and is symbolized by a horizontal line marked under the word to be pronounced in low pitch. The horizontal line has been shown as a sign of Anudatta in Rigveda Yajurveda and Atharva Veda as :—

अग्नि मीले—Udatta=1, इषे त्वोर्जे स्वा Anudatta २—१ ॥

तस्माद्यज्ञे स्वरवन्तं दिदृक्षन्त एव Swarit.

Swarit note denotes the combination of Udatta and Anudatta. It is expressed without any sign. Words are commonly used in Swarit and in pronouncing these words the sound remains just audible. It moves up and down hence Swarit represents half matra of Udatta and one and a half matra of Anudatta. The vertical and horizontal signs of Udatta and Anudatta respectively are used only on vowels and not on consonants. In Sam Veda, Udatta and Anudatta are expressed by writing figures over the words instead of vertical and horizontal lines as :—अग्न आ याहि ।

Four Notes — These three notes continued in practice for a very long period but in *Swarit* also the musicians faced a difficulty of distinguishing it from other notes. It did not produce any peculiarity of its own.

After a long span of time this difficulty of distinguishing *Swarit* from other notes was also removed by introducing *Prachaya* note in music, *Prachaya* note is also *one shruti* note. It differs from *swarit*. Prachaya is the note without any combination of udatta and Anudatta while swarit is the combination of both *udatta* and *anudatta* and is placed in middle of swarit note. This is one shruti note.

Five Notes—After the evolution of *Udatta, Anudatta, Swarit* and *Prachaya notes* the fifth note which came in practice is Nidhata which means the note of lowest pitch. It is described as :—

उदात्तश्चानुदात्तश्च स्वरित प्रचिते तथा ।
निघातश्चेति विज्ञेय: स्वरभेदस्तु पञ्चम: ॥

Seven Note—After the formation of above five notes we find the description of seven notes in *Vedic* literature. These seven notes are :—

उदात्त:, उदात्तर:, अनुदात्त: अनुदात्तर: स्वरित:,
स्वरितेय उदात्त: सो अन्येन विशिष्ठ: एक श्रुति: सप्तम: ॥

Udatta, Udattar, Anudatta, Anudattar Swarit, Swarit in the beginning of *Udatta* and one *Shruti* note.

After the formation of these 7 swaras, the arrangement of shrutis in them is as follows :—

The first swara (note) was of three shrutis. Hence taking this idea into consideration every note is provided with three shrutis each.

The middle note (Prachaya) is of one shruti only and is made of four shruti after adding 3 shrutis, and after that a space for 9 shrutis on both sides (up and down) is left for 3 notes on each side. According to some of the *granthas* when we came to know the movement of sound from lower octave to upper octave, we see that the fibres of the throat nerves around the voice box expands and contracts. the *loose nerves* down to pronounce the sound of *Anudatta* notes and as the sound moves upward the volume of the sound grows sharp and there is a tension in the throat nerves.

Patanjali has explained that the positions of throat for pronouncing vowels to be divided into 3 i.e. upper, middle and lower and a musician should pronounce *Udatta* from upper, *Anudatta* from lower and *Swarit* from the middle parts. In pronouncing *Udatta* note there is in nerves, sharpness in sound and contraction in throat and in pronouncing *Anudatta* note the throat is relaxed so that sweetness in sound and expansion of throat occurs.

Taking the above views of Patanjali into consideration, we have made the sound double by providing 22 shrutis from lower octave to upper octave when the sound raised upward the first note becomes of four shrutis, second of three shrutis and the third of two shrutis and assembles with the middle note of 4 shrutis, and when the second portion including middle note of 13 shrutis is further divided on the basis of sound, the first middle note becomes of 4 shrutis, second of 3 shrutis and the third of two shrutis and the remaining 4 shrutis are given to last upper note.

Now we fix these notes in another way. Previously the notes were divided in relation to the middle note, but now they are being fixed separately by uniting the middle note with the first part. From below the first note being of 4 *shrutis*, second of 3 *shrutis* and the third of 2 *shrutis* and the middle note 4 *shrutis* is kept fixed. In the 2nd part first note is of 4 *shrutis*, second of 3 *shrutis* and third of two *shrutis* is kept. Both of these methods have been shown on the basis of seven notes divided on 22 shrutis. The consequent notes after it became as *Kurshta, Prathama, Dwitya, Tritiya, Chaturtha, Mandra* and *Attiswara*.

Comparison of Vedic Notes and Saman Chants

Vedic Notes	*Saman Chants*
1. Udatta	1. Krushta
2. Udattar	2. Prathama
3. Anudatta	3. Dwitya
4. Anudattar	4. Tritiya
5. Swarit	5. Chaturtha
6. Swarit in beginning of Udatta	6. Mandra
7. One Shruti	7. Attiswara

After the above names the following names were fixed for the songs.

In the times of Panini the *Shadaj Rishabh Gandhar, Madhyam, Pancham, Dhaiwat* and *Nishad* had already been started. The co-relation between these two types of *note* is shown as follows on the basis of *Music of India* by Herbert A. Popley.

The correlation of these notes of the 'Saman Chant' with the notes of the secular or instrumental scale is another step in the process of this Inter-relationship of voice and instrument. We find evidence of this correlation, as early as the *RIKPRATHISAKHYA* in the statement that the Yama (Liturgical Scale) is the Swara (Instrumental). As we have seen the *Saman Scale* was conceived as a downward series and the instrumental scale as an upward series. The names used for the instrumental scale in the ancient books are those in use today, all over India. The clue to the interrelation of the two scales is found in the identification of *Prathama* and *Gandharva*. With this we get the two scales as follows, each forming a Saptaka or cluster of seven.

Saman	*Secular*
	Nishadha
	Dhaivata
	Panchama
Krushta	Madhyama
Prathama	Gandharva
Dwitya	Rishabha
Tritiya	Shadaja
Chaturtha	Nishadha
Mandra	Dhaivata
Attiswara	Panchama

It shows that the *Shadaj*, Rishabh, Gandhar, Madhyam Pancham, Dhaivat and Nishad Notes are associated with the *Krushta, Prathama, Dwitya, Tritiya, Chaturtha, Mandra* and *Attiswara*. But on account of convenience of pronouncing them with ease, only the first letter of each is taken as the symbol of the whole note. In this way we obtained the chain of notes as Sa, Re, Ga, Ma, Pa, Dha, Nee.

Sadhaja	Sa	Panchama	Pa
Rishabha	Re	Dhaivata	Dha
Gandhara	Ga	Nishada	Nee
Madhyama	Ma	Shadaja	Sa

This chain of note is very closely connected with the sound produced through our throats.

Aims of Swaras (Notes)

The word Swara is used in various forms to express various aims.

(i) According to Sanghitopanishad, Brahman Shiksha Shastra, Bharat Natya Shastra, Pratishakhya, Riktantra and Katantra etc. the word swara is used for the vowels pronounced without help of the consonantal variation.

(ii) In music literature the *swara* is used to express the notes—Shadaja, Rishabha, Ghandhara, Madhyama, Panchama, Dhaivata and Nishada.

(iii) Pingal Shastra explains that swara is used for representing the number seven due to popularity of seven Shadaja, Krushta and Udattas etc.

(iv) Swara is also used for the breathing air passing through two nostrils.

(v) In *Vedic Vangay*, swara is also used for *sun* and also for Udatta, Anudatta and Swarit.

(vi) Swara is sometimes used for *Somrassa.* *Shri* and *Pashu* (Animal etc.)

(vii) Swara is the name of *Pranava* or *Onkar.*

Seven Swaras on the Basis of Number—On account of prominence of *Shadaj* or Krushta etc. the word note is used for seven. This idea is given in *Chhanda Shastra* of *Pingal.*

Prastar contains seven *Ganas* and the half part is derived from *Arya Chhanda.*

Indian culture shows the prominence of seven as follows :—

1. The days of a year have been divided into 52 weeks of seven days each.
2. The rays of the sun are of seven colours.
3. The prominent stars are Sapta Rishis. It is a constelation of seven.
4. At the time of marriage the new couple in Hindu mythology takes seven rounds around fire.

Source of Notes

The names of notes have been given on the basis of Jatis which were popular before the times of Panini. They have been described by Bharat in Bharat Natya Shastra.

1. Madhyaodichya	5. Panchami	9. Shadaj Kechaki
2. Nadayanti	6. Gandharudichiyava	10. Shadajodischayavati
3. Gandhar Panchami	7. Arshibhi	11. Karmarvi
4. Dhaivati	8. Nishadi	12. Andhari

13. Madhyama	15. Rakta Gandhari	17. Kechiki
14. Gandhari	16. Shadajee	18. Shadaj Madhyama

The above 18 Jatis are associated with seven notes in the following manner:—

1. *Shadaja* : *Shadaj* Shadaj Kecheki, Shadajodichiyavati

2. *Reshabha* : *Arshibhi*

3. *Gandhara* : *Gandhar Panchami*, Gandharidichiyava
   Gandhari Rakta Gandhari

4. *Madhyama* : *Madhyama*, Madhyamaodichiyava

5. *Panchama* : *Panchami*

6. *Dhaivata* : *Dhaivati*

7. *Nishada* : *Nishadi*

The Achievements of Notes

(1) From the Tan Swara of first note we become familiar with the ascent and descent. At the time of Pranayam we take the air in the descent and throw it out in ascent.

(2) The magnitude and area of expansion of sound depend on the volume of the opening of the mouth at the time of producing sound. Higher the volume of mouth, greater is the dispersion of sound and in reverse the lesser volume of mouth requires the more tension in pitch of the sound.

```
4 S 3 R 2 G 4 M 4 P 3 D 2 N  Shadaj grama
4 P 3 D 2 N 4 S 3 R 2 G 4 M
4 S 3 R 2 G 4 M 3 P 2 D 4 N  Madhyam grama
4 S 3 R 2 G 4 M 4 P 3 D 2 N
```

(3) The first and second arrangements shown in chart produce the natural scale of old times by making Sa as basic note i.e. Shadaj Gram.

```
4 P 3 D 2 N 4 S 3 R 2 G 4 M
```

(4) When scale is made by supposing Pa as Sa the scale of Madhyam Gram is clearly visible because Pancham itself becomes of three shrutis.

```
4 S 3 R 2 G 4 M | 4 P 3 D 2 N
        G 4 M     4 P 3 D 2 N
```

(5) The scale of the second alternative draws a clear picture of both parts of octave i.e. the first note of first part becomes Sa i.e. Sa Re Ga Ma and that of second becomes Pa i.e. Pa Dha Nee Sa. This scale is also kept fit with the first scale of Shadaj Gram. 4 S 3 R 2 G 4 M

(6) From the above we conclude that the harmony of Shadaja Madhyam is the best, because it naturally resembles with the male and female sounds.

```
        ____
        |   |                    Wadi Swara   Samwadi Swara
P D N S R G M                     P——————————S
        |   |                     S——————————M
        ____
```

Fixation of Pitch of 'Sa' Note

The study of Indian Music literature does not convey a clear picture of the pitch of sound of 'Shadaj' note (Middle 'c'). According to *Natya Shastra* of *Bharat Muni* and *Sangeet Ratnakara* of Sharangadeva, the musician has to depend on the sound from the voice box. There is no definite rule for tuning the strings. In fact it is not difficult to measure the pitch *shadaj* note of human voice by an instrument like flute. Only the measurement of length, diameter and the extent of hole may enable a musician to fix up the position of notes.

In Sangeet Ratnakara and other medieval music literature, the sound of notes has been fixed up along with the names of the notes, their colour and gods and also the names of birds and animals whose sound resemble with that of the sound of notes. These *granthas* have supposed that the sound of human span of life is a true measure of the sound of notes such as :—

Note	Sa	Re	Ga	Ma	Pa	Dha	Nee
Life Span	70	60	50	40	30	20	10

We are intending to fix the sound of *Shadaj* according to the age group of human-beings. In olden days the human age was normally about 200 years and the structure of body and the pitch of sound depended on the height of the body.

If we fix up the basic notes on the basis of age group which were fixed up in olden days on the basis of *shruti* and sound, we get the scale of notes as follows :—

4 Sa	3 Ra	2 Ga	4 Ma	3 Pa	2 Dha	4 Nee=22
70	60	50	40	30	20	10

This scale resembles with that of *Madhyam Gram* of Bharata.

But the notes which are fixed according to the foreign literature are suitable to modern conditions of human life.

Notes with Shrutis	4 Pa	3 Dha	2 Nee	4 Sa	3 Re	2 Ga	4 Ma=22
Life Span	70	60	50	40	30	20	10

According to the above scale the sound of 10 year-old child resembles that of "*Madhyam note*" (*F*). If Ma note is supposed to be the sound of 10-year child, then our scales which are fixed according to foreign literature prove correct.

The sound of Shadaj resembles that of a man of 40 years. The western musicians recognized this sound as middle 'C' note. It means middle 'C' of today is correct according to the throat voice of man of 40 years and should be recognized as the sound of Shadaj.

Development of Universal Scale

After the formation of scale of music we are going to describe the way of development of this scale in the neighbouring countries like China, Iran and Arab where our trade and commerce were flourishing on a large scale. Out of the vast history of development of music, we are attempting to delineate only a portion which is more concerned with our music scale.

59

China

Quintal Pentatonic—The earliest scale on record may be said to have been the incomplete form of the basic scale, i. e. the 5 notes ascending major scale (Odava) or what I would call the Chinese quintal of the cycle of fifths.

The Chinese Quintal Pentatonic Ascending :—

C 9/8	D 9/8	E 32/27	G 9/8	A
Sa	Re	Ga	Pa	Dha

The characteristic intervals of this ascending quintal pentatonic scale (Bhoop) are the major tones and the quintal minor Third or trihe mitone, as can be seen from the second mode/murachhana, of this Chinese pentatonic.

Second mode of Quintal Pentatonic ascending :—

D	Tone	E	Min Third	G	Tone	A	Min Third	C
Re	9/8	Ga	32/27	Pa	9/8	Dha	32/27	Sa

The division of the major-tone into two semi-tones caused the tetrachord of the quintal pentatonic to be changed later in to the chromatic genius of the Greek system.

The ascending series of the perfect fifths C—G—D—A—E—B can never attain the perfect fourth F nor the upper octave C. The fourth and the octave can not, therefore, enter in to the scheme of the quintal pentatonic and hence the absence of the semi-tone.

Helmholtz's view that early civilizations tended to avoid the semi-tone, has no basis, in fact as we shall further see when we come to the equally ancient 5 note descending minor scale, which I call the up turned pentatonic.

In Pre-Buddhistic period, which may be called quintal age there was no knowledge of *the harmonic major. Third* (*Swayambhu Gandhar*) : all scales, including that of Pathagoras (570—500 B.C.) were based on quintal intervals, that is, built only by means of the artificial series of ascending fifths or descending fourths, and of descending fifths or ascending fourths. Though Gautama Buddha (563—483 B. C.) lived across the two centuries, the Quintal Age may be said to have ended with the close of the sixth century B.C. and the Tertian Age began at the dawn of the fifth century B.C.

From the times of the legendary Ling Lun (c. 2700 B.C.) who cut twelve bamboo pipes into a chain of perfect fifths, down to the days of King Fang (40 B. C.) who extended the cycle of quintal Lu's to sixty, the consistent Chinese tradition has been the practical 5-note quintal pentatonic.

This quintal structure of the incomplete Basic Scale has also survived in India in the form of Bhoop, as in Scotland, Ireland and other parts of the world. Derived from a series of fifths, the Chinese quintal pentatonic is based on the cyclic principle.

The Upturned Pentatonic—The other incomplete form of the basic scale is the descending 5 note minor scale of Egyptian Origin, corresponding to the modern Indian mode *Gunakali* which I called the upturned Pentatonic. It is based on enharmonic tetraehords or rather on descending fourths. The perfect fourth closing upon the quintal major-third (diatone) brings about the quintal semitone (Limma) in this descending Pentatonic.

60

The Egyptian upturned minor pentatonic conjunct, descending :—

Diatone	Limma	Diatone	Diatone	Limma
A	F	E	C	B
Ma	Re k	Sa	Dha k	Pa

The descending Indian minor-pentatonic Odava-Gunkali of the post-Buddhistic Tertian period is the exact upside down image of the later day Indian-ascending major-pentatonic Odava-Behaga. In both these scales each tetrachord consists of a major-third and a semitone. Obtained mainly by the ear-method, the harmonic division of the Indian upright pentatonic Odava-Behaga is based on the divisive principles.

Indian Odava-Behaga, Upright Major-Pentatonic ascending :—

	Maj-Third		Semi			Maj-Third		Semi	
C	E1		F	G		B1		C	
5/4	16/15		9/8	5/4				16/15	
Sa	Ga		Ma	Pa		Nee		Sa	

Indian Odava-Gunakali, Upturned Minor-Pentatonic ascending :—

	Maj-Third		Semi			Maj-Third		Semi	
e_1	C		B_1 9/8	A_1		F		E_1	
	5/4		16/15			5/4		16/15	
Sa	Dhak		Pa	Ma		Re k		Sa	

Though based on the major-third when traced from its descending top initial, the Egyptian upturned pentatonic always sounds minor in relation to its lower tonic octave hence the unscientific origin of the Egyptian upturned pentatonic later known as the Greek Scale of Olympos.

The three pentatonic scales are best studied when placed in juxtaposition. They are the Chinese quintal pentatonic, the Graeco-Egyptian upturned pentatonic and the Indian upright pentatonic.

C	C	C
Min-Third	Maj-Third	B_1 Maj-Third
A	C	G
G	B	G
Min-Third	A	F
E	Maj-Third	E_1 Maj-Third
D	F	C
C	E	

The Chinese Quintal Pentatonic (ascending). | The Graeco-Egyptian upturned pentatonic (descending) | The Indian upright pentatonic (ascending)

Of the three scales described above the Chinese pentatonic is the most ascending phase in the initial development of Bharata's Universal basic scale.

61

Notes on String Length

The idea of the notes on the length of string was known even in Bronze Age from 3000 B.C. onwards—as in Sumer, Babylon, Egypt that if we lay of 1/2 of the vibrating string or 1/2, of the 1/2 of it, the remaining length will sound the tonic Octave (Tar Sa) or the perfect fourth (Madhyam).

And later in Iron Age from 1000 B.C. onwards it is also on record that after the quintal thinkers like Long Lum, a Pythagoras, the Persian thinkers like Archytas, Plato (400 B.C.) and Didmus had already known that if we lay of 1/2 or 1/3 or 1/4 or 1/5 of the vibrating strings, the remaining length (1/2 or 2/3 or 3/4 or 4/5) will sound the tonic octave (Tar Sa) or the perfect fifth (Pancham), or the perfect fourth (Madhyam or the perfect harmonic major-third (Antara or Tambara Gandhar) respectively.

So, it fell to the historical lot of Bharata who was the first quintal Terhan scale maker, to discord the Pythagorian and other quintal scales.

The Basic Scale : Penultimate Stage

Sa-Grama of Bharata (5th-4th Cent. B.C.)

Bharata in his *Natya Shastra* speaks first of Sa-Grama, the older form of the Basic Scale, as being more symmetrical in the two tetrachords, thereby appearing to uphold a sequence which to my mind is an imperfect double-scale of bi-centric tonality. Bharata was the first to use in his scales the three diatonic intervals, namely, the major-tone, the minor-tone and the diatonic semitone.

Sa-Grama of Bharata, Bi-centric Basic Scale, Ascending Disjunction :

Maj-tone		Min-tone		Semi		Maj-tone		Min-tone		Semi	
C		D		E_1		F		G		A		B_1	C
	9/8		10/9		16/15				9/8		10/9	16/15
Sa		Re		Ga		Ma		Pa		Dha	Nee	Sa

HIGH DETERMINANT   HIGH DETERMINANT

As the note A is the perfect fifth of D, the two tetrachords having repetitive sequences are symmetrical and congruent.

To be correct, the delimitant or the sixth note of the scale, instead of being a high quintal A, should have been a low tertian A_1. The Sa-Grama is bi-centric, since it suggests two key-centres : C as well as G.

THE BASIC SCALE...........FINAL STAGE

Ma-Grama of *Bharata* (5th—4th Cent. B.C.)

Bharata's Ma-Grama finally provided the only perfect Universal Basic Scale of *Unicentric Tonality*, about 2000 years before Zarlino advocated the superiority of this scale in the West in 1558 A.D. Zarlino, however, had wrongly called it the Ptolemaic Sequence by mistaking the ascending order of one of Ptolemy's many descending permutations of the Green Dorian. To my mind, Zarlino was unaware of the fact that, unlike Pythagorean sequence, Ptolemy's sequence was irreversible. Bharata's 2400-year old 7-note Basic Scale has since not been and cannot possibly be improved upon.

Musicologists, who had no knowledge of the ancient Indian melodic system of music, had drawn the wrong conclusion that the Basic Scale was the exclusive product of the Western harmonic system of the 16th century.

The Basic Scale has a high quintal determinant D and a low tertian delimitant A_1. The high quintal determines the unicentric tonality of the scale and the tonic key-centre C, while the low tertian delimitant A inhibits the emergence of the second tonality of G-key. Bharata was the first to fix the intonation of the elusive tertian A_1.

The Ma-Grama Basic Scale is *unicentric* Because it is the only scalic tabulation that inhibits the secondary tonality of G or F besides that of the central C; also, it makes the correct harmonic division of the octave into the pentachord C—G and the tetrachord G—C.

The Universal Basic Scale of Unicentric Tonality, ascending.

Maj-tone		Min-tone	Semi	Disjunction		Min-tone	Maj-tone	Semi
C	D	E_1	F		G	A_1	B_1	C.
9/8	10/9	16/15		9/8		10/9	9/8	16/15
Sa	Re	Ga	Ma		Pa	Dha	Nee	Sa
HIGH DETERMINANT					HIGH DETERMINANT			

Cyclic, Equipartitive, Algebraic and Harmonic Principles

While the Natural Law of Harmonic Series and the Law of Vibrations were discovered by Marin Mersenne in 1636 A.D., the Chinese, Egyptian, Indian, Greek, Arabic and the Persian systems of music were arrived at solely by means of string lengths and the Ear Method. But they all obtained the same results. Having evolved an algebraic formula to deduce the intervalic values of Bharata's descriptive shrutis, I would call the Indian system an Algebraic Method.

While the Ear Method was a common factor in all the systems, the Chinese system used the cyclic principle; the Egyptian and the Greek systems used the equipartitive principle; the Indian system, the algebraic principle; the Arabic and the Persian systems used both the cyclic and the equipartitive principles to arrive at approximate quintal-equivalents of just tertian intervals.

All these systems were based either on the cyclic, equipartitive, algebraic or divisive principles, and can now be tested with accuracy against the modern harmonic laws of accoustics. Of the three methods, the Indian division system or the algebraic method was the most accurate before the advent of the modern harmonic analyser.

Afterwards the quintal Dorial of Phythagorus descending was approved.

	Sem		Tone	Tone		Tone		Sem		Tone		Tone	
	E		F	G		A		B		C		D	E
Tone		Tone	Sem	Tone	Tone		Tone		Sem				
C		D	E	F	G		A		B		C		

VIBRATION SYSTEM

"The Algebraic and Harmonic setting of notes on strings were again brought under check through Vibration System, while the natural law of Harmonic series and the law of vibrations were discovered by Marin Mersenne in 1636 A.D., the Chinese, Egyptian, Indian,

63

Greek, Arabic and the Persian systems of music were arrived at solely by men by means of the *'string lengths'* and the *'ear'* method. But they all obtained the same results. Having evolved an *algebraic formula* to deduce, the intervalic values as Bharata's descriptive *shrutis*, I would call the Indian system an *Algebraic method*."

(These informations are collected from three Monographs on Music by Anti Sher Lobo and Hira Lal Kapadia.)

Method of Finding out Number of Vibrations :—

The method of calculation of finding out the value of middle C (Sa), first 240 and then 256.

The System of obtaining middle C

Measure Pitch By counting Vibrations.

As this wheel rotates each tooth strikes the metal strip and makes it vibrate setting up sound waves. The speed of the rotation can be varied. The number of teeth multiplied by the number of rotations per second gives us the number of vibrations per second (V.P.S.) of the strip. The V.P.S. of the strip is also the frequency of the note heard.

If the wheel has 128 teeth and rotates twice in one second we shall hear a note with 256 vibrations per second. This frequency or the number of vibrations per second is the same as that which is produced when the note called middle C on a piano is struck.

If we play middle C and then miss the next six white notes and play the seventh we shall be playing a note with exactly twice as many vibrations per second as middle C. If we repeat the process on the piano and then starting again at middle C, work down the piano in the same manner, every note we play will be a C. From the information given, you should be able to *check* on the number of vibrations per second necessary to produce each of the C. S.

In the siren the wheel has a number of holes which pass across the nozzle of a pipe blowing out air. Each puff through a hole is a vibration and so a note is sounded. The speed of the wheel can be regulated and from the speed of the wheel and the number of holes in it, the number of vibrations per second in the harmony of the note can be calculated.

GRADUAL DEVELOPMENT IN INDIAN MUSIC SCALE

After the development of the Chinese music, upto modern times, no one has divided the notes on 22 *shruti* interval that remained popular with the theoreticians only. From the very beginning, the notes have been divided into 24 *shrutis*. For example the Chinese have shown the *shruti* interval as follows :—

4 Shrutis	9/8	=	204 cents
5 Shrutis	32/27	=	294 cents
6 Shrutis	6/5	=	316 cents

Now they have been divided on the basis of 1200 cents such as :—

$$1200/22 \quad = \quad 54\tfrac{1}{2} \quad \times 4 \quad = \quad 218+4 \quad = \quad 222 \text{ cents}$$
$$1200/24 \quad = \quad 50 \quad \times 4 \quad = \quad 200+4 \quad = \quad 204 \text{ cents}$$

These Chinese houses supposed our *shruti* interval as unequal and made all the calculations on the basis of 24 *shrutis*.

Bharata was the first man who used his scales in three diatonic intervals, namely, the major tone, the diatonic and semitone.

The three diatonic intervals are :

(a) The major tone   9/8 or 204 cents, Chaturshruti
(b) Minor tone   9/10 or 182 cents, Thrishruti
(c) The diatonic semi-tone. 17/15 or 112 cents, Dwishruti

If we wish to take 22 shrutis as equally tempered micro-intervals as some musicologists reckon them, like each equal unit would have the ratio 129/125 or 54.5 cents. This is not acceptable to any other country.

The old Tamil Granthas show that 24 *Shrutis* were popular in 3rd and 4th century A.D. as well.

"The Shruti or microtonal interval is a division of the semi-tone but not necessarily an equal division. It is an interesting fact that we find in Greek music the counterpart of many things which are in Indian music and we have a good deal of information about the development of Greek music. We may look at those to get help from that source in our study of Indian music. The ancient Greek scale divided the octave into 24 Small Intervals while the traditional Indian practice is to recognize 22 in the Octave. Rao Sahib Abraham Pandita, a South Indian music scholar who has made a very close study of Tamil books of the second and third centuries of our era supports the view that in South India the octave was also divided into 24 equal intervals."

(Music of India—Herbet A Popley)

It seems that after the Mahabharata Age, Indian music might have adopted 24 *shrutis* in an octave under the influence of foreign music and that very scale might have continued in the later stage.

In 5th century A.D. in times of Bharat Natya Shastra the author might have tried to re-expose the old principle and pointed out the *Gram Murchhanas* supposing 22 *Shrutis* as his base. After Bharata, in the Buddha period, music was in a prosperous condition. The musicians and dancers used to sing, dance and play on musical instruments during religious performances in other countries as well. Though we do not possess any approved *grantha* on this subject of that time, yet we can estimate that there was a practice of 24 *Shrutis* in an octave at that time and the frets on *Veena* also were fixed in the same period.

In 13th century A.D. when Sharengdeva wrote his book Sangeeta Ratnakara, he followed the system of *Gram Murchhanas* which were laid down by Bharata. He did not mention the frets on the Veena.

After the 13th Century A.D. the two types of notes in Indian music were *Utara* and *Chada* which were called half tone and sharp notes respectively. In this scale too, we get the mention of 24 *Shrutis*. Every one appreciated the idea and adopted it. Ma of full tone as Ma sharp note as is also seen in SVARAMELAKALANIDHI.

Though the old seven shuddha swaras and the shuddha scale formed thereby have, doubtless, become obsolete, yet we have now Sa and Pa, as Shuddha (or better, Prakrithi) Swaras, in as much as they are fixed or admit of no varieties at all, while Re, Ga, Ma, Dha, Nee are Vikrit Swaras in as much as each of them admits of two clear varieties viz. Komal and Tivra i.e. flat and sharp. These modern shuddha, vikrita swaras, twelve in number, may be tabulated thus:

Sa	Re¹	Re²	Ga¹	Ga²	Ma¹	Ma²	Pa	Dha¹	Dha²	Nee¹	Nee²
1	2	3	4	5	6	7	8	9	10	11	12

Bharata Natya Shastra was written in the 5th Century A.D. and Sangeeta Ratnakara in the 13th Century. Both these books are athenticated of the old music literature. After that we have Ragatarangini by Kavi Lochan in 15th Century A.D.

Sangeet Parijata by Ahobal in 17th Century and Hriday Kautuk and Hriday Prakash by Hridaya Narayan Deva in later half of the same century and Raga-Tatva Vibodha by Pt. Shrinivas had been written. These are the prominent *Granthas* of Medieval Age. All these *Granthas* follow Sangeet Ratnakara for seven notes. According to these *Granthas* the notes have been fixed as follows :—

              Sa   C   on   the   4th   Shruti
              Re   D   on   the   7th   Shruti
              Ga   E   on   the   9th   Shruti
              Ma   F   on   the   13 th   Shruti
              Pa   G   on   the   17th   Shruti
              Dha A   on   the   20th   Shruti
              Nee B   on   the   22nd   Shruti

But leaving Bharata Natya Shastra and Sangeet Ratnakara, other *Granthas* support the idea of variation in *Shrutis* under the influence of foreign music literature. In the history of Indian Music literature Sangeet Parijata is the first book to explain the fixation of Swaras on the length on the string but whatever method of treatment is given in Sangeet Parijata is also followed by Ling Lun, Pythagorus, Archytas and Plato in 1000 B.C. Besides this in 14th Century Amir Khusro made a Sitar with 3 Strings and fixed 14 Frets on it.

The interval between the frets was fixed on finger measures. This method was approved by British Government—

              4 soot = one finger
              2 fingers = one inch
              12 inches = one foot

The notes thus fixed were on 24 *shrutis* on the principle of 22 *shrutis* is the basic principle and has been accepted as universal scale by all.

DEVELOPMENTS IN NORTH INDIAN MUSIC

First of all two distorted notes—Antar Gandhar and Kakli Nishad were made. After this the number of distorted notes changed from time to time. The Indian musicians accepted the use of 5 distorted notes on the basis of alien scale of notes. Some of the prominent granthas speak about the distorted notes as follows :—

	Grantha	*Fulltone Notes*	*Distorted Notes*	*Total*
1.	Sangeet Ratnakara	7	12	19
2.	Raga Vibodha	7	7	14
3.	Swarmela Kalanidhi	7	7	14
4.	Chatur Dandika Prakashika	7	5	12
5.	Sangeet Parijata	7	5	12

All the above granthas accepted old scale as their basic scale i.e. 4 Sa 3 Re 2 Ga 4 Ma 4 Pa 3 Dha 2 Nee.

Statement showing Shuddha and Vikrit Swaras.

Shrutis	Notes taken from					
	Ratnakara	Ragavibodha	Swar Mela Kalanidhi	Chaturadandi Prakashika and Sangita Saramrita	Sangita Parijata	Current Indian Music
1.						
2.						
3.	Chyuta Shadja	Mridu Shadja	Chyuta Shadja Nishada	—	—	—
4.	Shuddha Shadja	Shuddha Shadja	Shuddha Shadja	Shuddha Shadja	Shuddha Shadja	Shuddha Shadja
5.	Kaishika Shadja	—	—	—	—	—
6.	Antara Shadja	—	—	—	Komala Rishabha	Komala Rishabha
7.	Shuddha Rishabha	Shuddha Rishabha	Shuddha Rishabha	Shuddha Rishabha	Shuddha Rishabha or Purva Gandharva	—
8.	Vikrita Rishabha	—	—	—	—	Shuddha Rishabha
9.	Shuddha Gandhara	Shuddha Gandhara	Shuddha Gandhara or Pancha Shruti Rishabha	Shuddha Gandhara	Shuddha Gandhara or Tivratara Rishabha	—
10.	Sadharana Gandhara	Sadharana Gandhara	Sadharana Gandhara or Shatshruti Rishabha	Sadharana Gandhara	Tivratama Rishabha or Tivra Gandhara	Komala Gandhara
11.	Antara Gandhara	Antara Gandhara	Antara Gandhara	Antara Gandhara	—	Shuddha Gandhara
12.	—	Mridu Madhyama	Chyuta Madhyam Gandhara	—	—	—
13.	Shuddha Madhayama	Shuddha Madhayama	Shuddha Madhyama	Shuddha Madhyama	Shuddha Madhyama	Shuddha Madhyama

Shru-tis	Ratanakara	Ragavibodha	Swaramola Kalanidhi.	Chaturadandi Prakashika and Sangita Saramrita	Sangita Parijata	Current Indian music
14.	Kaishika Madhyama	—	—	—	—	—
15.	Vikrita Madhyama	—	—	Varali Madhyama	Tivratara Madhyama	Tivra Mad yama
16.	Madhyama Grama Pan-chama	Mridu Pan-chama	Chyuta Pan-chama Ma dhayama	—	—	—
17.	Shuddha Panchama or Vikrita M.G. Pan-chama.	Shuddha Panchama	Shuddha Panchama	Shuddha Panchama	Shuddha Panchama	Shuddha Panchama
18.	Madhyama-- Grama Dhaivata	—	—	—	—	—
19.	—	—	—	—	Komala Dhaivata	Komala Dhaivata
20.	Shuddha Dhaivata or Vikrita M.G. Dhaivata	Shuddha Dhaivata	Shuddha Dhaivata	Shuddha Dhaivata	Shuddha Dhaivata or Purva Nishada	—
21.	—	—	—	—	—	Shuddha Dhaivata
22.	Shuddha Nishada	Shuddha Nishada	Shuddha Nishada or Pancha-shruti Dhaivata	Shuddha Nishada	Shuddha Nishada or Tiva-ratara Dhaivata	—
1.	Kaishika Nishada	Kaishika Nishada	Kaishika Nishada or Shatshru-ti Dhaivata	Kaishika Nishada	Tivratama Dhaivata or Tivra Nishada	Komala Nishada
2.	Kakali Ni-shada	Kakali Ni-shada	Kakali Ni-shada	Kakali Ni-shada	—	Shuddha Nishada
3.						
4.						

After Sarang Deva, started the North Indian system of music. The Shuddha and Vikrita Swaras were known as *Utara* and *Chada* with the following arrangement :

Sa	Achal	Fixed
Re	Utara	Komal
Re	Chada	Tivra
Ga	Utara	Komal
Ga	Chada	Tivra
Ma	Utara	Komal
Ma	Chada	Tivra
Pa	Achal	Fixed
Dha	Utara	Komal
Dha	Chada	Tivra
Nee	Utara	Komal
Nee	Chada	Tivra

All the three notes-full tone, half tone and sharp not were not in practice in those days. Ma Shuddha was taken as Ma Komal or Ma Utara. Since the time when Mohammad Raza prohibited Rag-Ragini system by adopting Bilawal Thata as Shuddha Thata, we see a change in old and new scale system. This variation is constantly running from the times of Rag-Ragini system but no one took pains to give it a black and white shape and people faced difficulty to furnish the old shruti interval on Veena and especially when frets were fixed to the instrument.

When V.N. Bhatkhande made the new system of music and adopted Bilaval Thata as Shuddha Thata, the five scales had already been formed. They were as follows :

(i) On the basis of sound and shrutis :

4 Sa   3 Re   2 Ga   4 Ma   3 Pa   2 Dha   4 Nee=22

(ii) Scale on the basis of English Literature :

4 Pa   3 Dha   2 Nee   4 Sa   3 Re   2 Ga   4 Ma=22

(iii) The scale by dividing the Octave into 2 parts :

4 Sa   3 Re   2 Ga   4 Ma   4 Pa   3 Dha   2 Nee=22

(iv) Shuddha scale with Antar Gandhar and Kakli Nee :

2 Sa   3 Re   4 Ga   2 Ma   4 Pa   3 Dha   4 Nee=22

(v) Scale supposing Nee as Sa:

2 Nee   4 Sa   3 Re   2 Ga   4 Ma   4 Pa   3 Dha=22

When V.N. Bhatkhande made his own scale, he reversed the scale which was made supposing Nee as Sa:

2 Nee   4 Sa   3 Re   2 Ga   4 Ma   4 Pa   3 Dha
Sa 4   Re 3   Ga 2   Ma 4   Pa 4   Dha 3   Nee 2

Old Scale		Sa		Re	Ga			Ma				Pa		
1	2 3 4	5 6 7	8 9	10 11	12 13	14 15 16	17							
New Scale Sa			Re		Ga	Ma		Pa						

Dha   Nee
18   19   20   21   22
Dha   Nee

The fixation of notes on this ground, no doubt, followed the same shruti numbers bu it brought some changes in thatas i.e. the old scale was on the basis of Kafee Thata while th new one was fixed on the basis of Bilaval Thata. Out of these two scales the old prove more suitable for the Indian music.

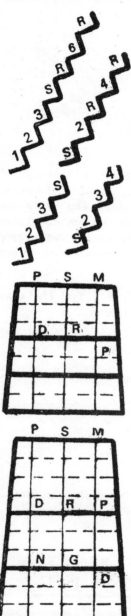

The proper use of shrutis is very essential in Indian music Without the use of Shrutis our classical music can show mere tunin or sounding. It fails to originate *Rasas* and to depict the clea picture of Ragas. The use of Shrutis is more useful than mer singing on notes. Shrutis play a prominent role in improvisation If the Shrutis are removed from Indian music then its structure wi also be destroyed. The only quality of Indian music is to expres the inner feelings through Shrutis.

1. Before comparing the old and new scales try to follow th following points :

(i) The sound increases in height and then arrives at a not because it reaches its fixed point from the back Shrutis.

(ii) Every distorted note originates in the basic note shruti i.e. in between R G N D Komal Swara and Ma Tivra. When Shruti are pronounced before some note they express only a part of nex note.

(iii) In improvisation when Shrutis next to a note are use they express the tone of next note.

For example in the old system, the musician raises his soun in ascending order to reach the basic note while in the new system the musician has to pass over his sound through Shrutis of bac notes i.e. to fix our sound we will have to fix our Sa note 1 2 3 S at touching first, second and third Shrutis but in the new system w will have to set our voice through Nee to fix a Sa note. N—Sa 2 3 4

2. In the old system each distorted note is formed in th Shrutis of same category,

1	2	3	4	5	6	7
			Sa	R		Re

but in the new system every distored note is formed in Shruti o back note.

1	2	3	4	5
S		R		Re

According to the old scale system Re komal is formed between Sa and Shuddha Re on Re Shrutis. In new system it is formed between Sa & Re Shuddha on Shrutis of Sa.

3. Both these cases seem unsuitable for Indian music. In modern scale such as Shrutis of Rishabha komal are tried to be touched by prolongation then this shrutis take

the form of Shadaja in place of Rishabha and the musician runs through the Shrutis of Shadaja.

Besides this the fixation of notes on first Shruti is unsuitable for freted instrumental music.

According to old scale the first fret of Sitar is set on the 4th Shruti on which Re and Dha of 2nd and 3rd Strings can be played but there is no fret for 'Pa' note on String No. 1 which is set on 5th Shruti from Ma.

In new scale, when Shruti of every note is supposed after Pa, Sa & Ma, the first fret is set on 5th Shruti and the Pa, Re and Dha of String Nos. 1, 2 and 3 are played well. But after that is the fret of 'Ga' on 7th Shruti. On this fret, no doubt, 'Ga' and 'Nee' of String No. 2 and 3 can be played but Dha note of String No. 1 is set on 4th Shruti from 'Pa' where there is no fret. It is difficult to an instrument according to 22 Shrutis. Hence the principle of 24 Shrutis is more convenient and useful.

Music Notes

71

10

New Scale Based on 24 Shrutis

Naghmate Asafi was written by Mohd. Raza of Patna in 1813. He supposed Bilaval Thata as Shuddha Thata, on the basis of 22 Shrutis. Shri V. N. Bhatkhande also followed the same but after that upto modern age all the musicians have been using 24 Shrutis in their vocal and instrumental music. The case of 22 Shrutis remained upto theory only. Hence to remove this difficulty a scale of 24 Shrutis is being formed. In forming this scale the following points have been taken into consideration :

1. The universal scale contains only two notes i.e. Full tone and half tone. We have introduced 3 notes—*Shuddha Komal* and *Tivra* as per views of Shri Bhatkhande.

2. The notes of the scale of Shri Bhatkhande are fixed on first Shruti which does not suit to the musician. We have followed the old scale and every note has been fixed on last Shruti. This has been done by putting *Antar Gandhar* and *Kakli Nee* in the scale. It is suitable to Bilaval Thata.

```
4    3    2    4    4    3    2
Sa   Re   Ga   Ma   Pa   Dha  Nee=22
Antar Gandhar & Kakli Nee
2    3    4    2    4    3    4
Sa   Re   Ga   Ma   Pa   Dha  Nee
```

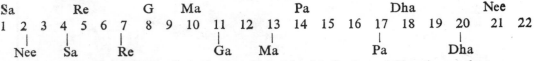

Every note is fixed on the last Shruti in this Scale and Shrutis are the same as in old scale system.

3. The two Shrutis which have been added to old system have been placed where there was no Shruti interval, for example the first Shruti in between Sa and *Re* Komal while other in between Pa and Dha Komal.

4. The names of the Shrutis which have been added are taken from Shrutis of Narda, for example *Sikka* Shruti between 'Sa' and *Re* Komal and *Shantha* Shruti between 'Pa' and *Dha* Komal.

5. In adopting 24 Shrutis in place of 22 Shrutis there is no difference in the length of strings. The interval between Sa of Madhya Octave and Sa of Upper Octave

(the same as in case of 22 Shrutis interval) has been divided into 24 intervals. This makes a very minute difference i.e. '4.5' Cents per Shruti interval. The Shruti interval in case of 22 Shrutis is 54.5 Cents while in case of 24 it is 50 Cents. This makes a difference of 4.5 Cents only. This difference puts no hindrance in Vocal and Instrumental music.

6. This scale effects neither Thatas nor notes of Ragas. Hence this scale suits to the Indian Vocal and Instrumental music both in theory and practice.

Old and Modern Scales

Shruti No.	Name of Shrutis	Present Music Scale according to Bilawal Thata	Old Music Scale according to present Kaffee Thata.	Old Music Scale according to Antar Gandhar and Kakli Nee
1.	Tivra	Sa		
2.	Kumodvati			Nee Kakli
3.	Manda			
4.	Chhandovati		Sa	Sa
5.	Dayavati	Re		
6.	Ranjani			
7.	Raktika	Ga	Re	Re
8.	Raudari			
9.	Krodhi		Ga	
10.	Vijrika	Ma		
11.	Parsarini			Ga Antra
12.	Preeti			
13.	Marjini		Ma	Ma
14.	Ksbiti	Pa		
15.	Rakta			
16.	Sandeepini			
17.	Alapine		Pa	Pa
18.	Madanti	Dha		
19.	Rohini			
20.	Ramya		Dha	Dha
21.	Ugra	Nee		
22.	Kumodvati		Nee	
1.				
2.				Nee Kakli

```
Old Scale        Sa      Re    Ga            Ma          Pa        Dha   Nee
          1  2  3  4  5  6  7  8  9  10  11  12  13  14  15  16  17  18  19  20  21 22
Modern Sa        Re        Ga    Ma            Pa              Dha           Nee
```

73

Shuddha and Vikrit Notes

Shruti No.	Name of Shrutis	Present Music Scale according to Bilawal Thata	Old Music Scale according to Antar Gandhar and Kakli Nee	Re Komal, Dha Komal and Ma Tivra
1.	Tivra	Sa Achal		
2.	Kumodvati			
3.	Manda	Re Komal		
4.	Chhandavati		Sa Achal	
5.	Dayavati	Re Shuddha	Re Komal	Re Komal
6.	Ranjani			
7.	Raktika	Ga Komal	Re Shuddha	
8.	Randhari	Ga Shuddha		
9.	Krodhi		Ga Komal	
10.	Vajrika	Ma Shuddha		
11.	Parsarni		Ga Shuddha	Antar Gandhar
12.	Preeti	Ma Tivra		
13.	Marjini		Ma Shuddha	
14.	Kshiti	Pa Achal		
15.	Rakta		Ma Tivra	Ma Tivra
16.	Sandeepini	Dha Komal		
17.	Alapini		Pa Achal	
18.	Madanti	Dha Shuddha	Dha Komal	Dha Komal
19.	Rohini			
20.	Ramya	Nee Komal	Dha Shuddha	
21.	Ugra	Nee Shuddha		
22.	Kshobini		Nee Komal	
1.	Tivra			
2.	Kumodvati		Nee Shuddha	Kakli Nee

Statement Showing Old and New Scales

Old Scale of 22 Shrutis			New Scale of 24 Shrutis	
1. Tivra				1. Tivra
2. Kumodvati	Nee Shuddha	Nee Shuddha		2. Kamodvati
3. Manda				3. Manda
4. Chhandovati	Sa Achal	Sa Achal		4. Chhandovati
5. Dayavati	Re Komal			5. Sikka
		Re Komal		6. Dayavati
6. Ranjini				7. Ranjini
7. Raktika	R Shuddha	Re Shuddha		8. Raktika
8. Roudri				9. Roudri
9. Krodhi	G Komal	Ga Komal		10. Krodhi
10. Vajrika				11. Vajrika
11. Parsarni	G Shuddha	Ga Shuddha		12. Parsarni
12. Preeti				13. Preeti
13. Marjini	M Shuddha	Ma Shuddha		14. Marjini
14. Kshiti				15. Kshiti
15. Rakta	M Tivra	Ma Tivra		16. Rakta
16. Sandeepini				17. Sandeepini
17. Alapini	Pa Achal	Pa Achal		18. Alapini
				19. Shantha
18. Madanti	Dha Komal	Dha Komal		20. Madanti
19. Rohini				21. Rohini
20. Ramya	Dha Shuddha	Dha Shush		22. Ramya
21. Ugra				23. Ugra
22. Kshobini	Nee Komal	Nee Komal		24. Kshobini

			Sa	Re	R	Ga	Ga	Ma	Ma	Pa	Dha
22. Shrutis	1	2 3	4	5	6 7	8 9	10 11	12 13	14 15	16 17	18 19 20

24. Shrutis	Nee	Sa	Re	Re	Ga	Ga	Ma	Ma	Pa	Dha

Nee

21	22	23	24
Dha	Nee		Nee

75

Statement Showing Shrutis on Notes

Name of Shrutis Old System	Notes	Name of Shrutis New System
Chhandovati	Sa Achal	Chhandovati
Dayavati	Re Komal	Dayavati
Raktika	Re Shddha	Raktika
Karodhi	Ga Komal	Karodhi
Parsarini	Ga Shuddha	Parsarini
Marjini	Ma Shuddha	Marjini
Rakta	Ma Tivra	Rakta
Alapini	Pa Achal	Alapini
Madanti	Dha Komal	Madanti
Ramya	Dha Shuddha	Ramya
Kshobini	Nee Komal	Kshobini
Kumodvati	NeeS huddha	Kumodvati

Statement Showing Numbers on Shrutis of Notes

Chhandovati	Sa Achal	2	Shrutis	Manda and Chhandovati
Raktika	Re Shuddha	4	Shrutis	Sika, Dayavati, Ranjini and Raktika
Parsarini	Ga Shuddha	4	Shrutis	Roudri, Krodhi Vajrika and Parsarini
Marjini	Ma Shuddha	4	Shrutis	Preeti, Marjini, Kshobini and Rakta
Alapini	Pa Achal	2	Shrutis	Sandeepini and Alapini
Ramya	Dha Shuddha	4	Shrutis	Shantha, Madanti, Rohini and Ramya
Kumovti	Nee Shuddha	4	Shrutis	Ugra, Ksho bini, Tivra and Kumodwati

Nee	Sa		Re			Ga	Ma		Pa		Dha		
1 2 3	4 5	6 7	8 9	10	11	12 13	14 15 16	17	18	19 20	21 22	23 24	

	Re		Ga			Ma		Dha		Nee

11

Octaves

The combination of 7 Notes is called Octave It includes all the natural and distorted notes in the difference of magnitude of sound right from the first shadaja to second shadaja. An Octave is borne out of the notes (Swaras) as notes from shrutis and shrutis from Nada (Sound). Octave contains 12 notes in all as follows :—

Natural notes	=	7
Halftone notes	=	4
Sharp note	=	1
Total :		12

On the basis of music literature Octaves are of 3 types :—

Three types of sound which come out of the body are—Lower, Medium and Upper Octaves. The centre of lower octave is heart, medium octave is throat and that of upper octave is sheers or head. (Sangeet Darpana)

The three types of sound ascend in magnitude in multiple of two from the previous one i.e.

Lower Octave	Medium Octave	Upper Octave
2 ,,	2 × 2	4 × 2
2 ,,	4	8

If we compare the origin of Nada in human body and Veena, we will know that in human body the sound of lower nada bears its origin in heart, medium nada in throat and upper nada in head but in Veena the case is just reverse i.e. in veena the lower nada bears its origin in upper most part, medium nada a bit lower and the upper nada in the lowest part of the Veena. (Sangeet Darpana)

The lower octave bears its origin in heart, medium in throat and upper in mind and every nada is just double than its lower one i.e. medium double than lower and the upper double than the medium octave. It can be understood as : the air pressure for the movement of upper octave is double than that of medium octave which itself requires double the pressure than that of lower octave for its movement. (Sangeet Parijat)

From the above we come to the conclusion that there are 3 Octaves—Lower, Medium and Upper. The stringed musical instruments also contain 3 Octaves. In some instruments a separate string is used for the Atimandra Saptaka (Double lower octaves). Some foreign musical instruments like Organ and Piano etc. contain 8 Octaves too. But according to human voice octaves are only of three types :—

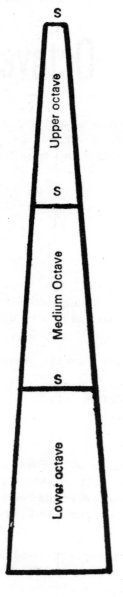

1. *Lower Octave*—The sound which is produced with the force of chest is called the sound of lower octave. It is slower and lighter than that of the sound of medium octave. The notes which are played on this Octave are Sa, Re, Ga, Ma, Pa, Dha, Nee.

2. *Medium Octave*—The sound which comes out of the throat without use of any force is called the sound of Medium octave and the notes which are called the medium octave notes are:—

Sa Re Ga Ma Pa Dha Nee

3. *Upper Octaves*—The sound which requires sufficient force to come out is called the sound of upper octave and the notes which are pronounced in that sound are called the notes of upper octave. Such as :—

Sa Re Ga Ma Pa Dha Nee. The position of upper octave is supposed to be in the mind or head. The pronunciation of the notes of upper octave exert force on mind and the fore side of ears.

Generally the musicians take their voice upto Ma note of lower octave only but some good musicians sing upto Sa note of lower octave also. In times of Akbar Swami Haridas and Tansen sang also in double lower octave. The buzzing and force of this type of singing was more than that of lower octave. The sound of medium and upper octave is doubled by higher but it lacks in buzzing and deepness.

Double Lower Octave— Sa Re Ga Ma Pa Dha Nee

Lower Octave— Sa Re Ga Ma Pa Dha Nee

Medium Octave—Sa Re Ga Ma Pa Dha Nee

Upper Octave—Sa Re Ga Ma Pa Dha Nee

Movement of 12 notes of an Octave

No.	Full Name	Short	Name	Category	Nature
1.	Shadaja	Sa	C	Achal	Fixed
2.	Rishabha	Re	b D	Komal	Half tone
3.	Rishabha	Re	D	Natural	Natural
4.	Gandhara	Ga	b E	Komal	Half tone
5.	Gandhara	Ga	E	Natural	Natural
6.	Madhyama	Ma	F	Natural	Natural
7.	Madhyama	Ma|	F	Tivra	Sharp
8.	Panchama	Pa	G	Achal	Fixed
9.	Dhaivata	Dha	b A	Komal	Half tone
10.	Dhaivat	Dha	A	Natural	Natural
11.	Nishada	Nee	b B	Komal	Halftone
12.	Nishada	Nee	B	Natural	Natural

12

Evolution of Thatas

The Gram-Murchhana System was prevalent in India before that system.

Grams are not difficult to be understood. A Gram is the note on the basis of voice of the sound of a musician. With the help of Gram a musician sing successfully. Even today the musician is asked about a note or the Gram to start with and sets his instrument accordingly.

All the three Grams—Shadaja, Madhyama and Gandhara of old days, are popular even today. Shadaja Gram was used for male voice, Madhyama Gram for female or the boys of 10 to 13 years age and Gandhara Gram for the students of teen age. The question of age does not affect sound of girls of any age.

After some practical experience the Gandhara Gram was totally prohibited for fear of spoiling the voice of throat. The learners were advised to have a rest so that their throats may set themselves automatically in teen age. Even today the students of teen age are advised to have a light practice or a complete rest.

First of all when the Theatres became popular in India, no lady was available for playing a female role, hence, the boys of 10 to 13 years age were given practice for playing ladies role on stage. But when their throat voice became heavier they were either replaced or were given medicines to bring their throat voice in order. This shows that Gandhara Gram was fixed in between Shadaja and Madhyama Gram. With the effect of heaviness in throat of boys in Madhyama Gram, the sound decreased towards the Shadaja Gram and at that point the previous note (Gandhara) was fixed for practice. It failed to sharpen the voice hence prohibited all together.

Gram-Murchhana

The description of Gram-Murchhana first of all is found in Bharat Natya Shastra. The authors of the following times have supported the principle. Sangeet Ratnakar depict the notes on shrutis according to their numbers and the movement of all the three Gramas. The musicians of the medieval age adopted three Gramas, Seven notes, 22 Shrutis, 2 Murchhanas and 49 Koot Tanas, but no one has clearly explained the Gram and no musician has widely explained the Gram Murchhana system because we do not get the systematic and vivid picture of sound historical facts of Gramas as yet.

Neither Pt. Vishnu Narain Bhat Khande nor Pt. Vishnu Digamber Paluskar has put forth any information about the principles of Gram-Murchhanas. Some of the proverb speak about Gram-Murchhanas as follows :

    1.   All the three Grams have been supposed on the basis of three Octaves.

GRAMS

Shadaj Gram

Madhyam Gram

Gandhar Gram

2. Gram denotes a village and Murchhana as lanes in it.
   (Marphul Nagmat By Th. Navab Ali Khan)

3. Grams are supposed on the basis of category of notes Natural, Half tone and Sharp, i.e.

   (i) Shadaja Gram—Full tone notes—Sa Re Ga Ma Pa Dha Nee

   (ii) Madhyam Gram—Sharp notes—Sa Re Ga Ma Pa Dha Nee

   (iii) Gandhar Gram—Half tone notes—Sa *Re Ga* Ma Pa *Dha Nee.*

If the musicians set their voice at Sa of Shadaja Gram, how will they be able to control their voices at Re of lower octave, for last Murchhana.

Moreover is it possible whether musicians who sing at Sa of Shadaja Gram, will sing successfully on Madhyam note and also is it essential to sing at Madhyam or Gandhar for Half tone or Tivra notes.

The Sangeet Ratnakar and the preceding granthas show that Shadaj and Madhyam Grams are only in practice now-a-days. Gandhar Gram has practically vanished and is sung in Gandharva Loka due to high pitch.

According to Bharat Natya Shastra Brahma asked Bharat to arrange and stage drama for encouraging Devas for battle against Asuras. Bharat trained his hundred sons but went to Brahma as he could not manage any female character for his drama. Brahma asked Indra to provide the court musicians and dancers to play the role of female character in the drama of Bharata.

This provision clarifies two points : Firstly the pitch of the female musicians who came from Indra's court, should have four notes higher than Shadaja (at Madhyam). The pitch of the male musicians, of Indra's court, was two notes higher than the pitch of singers of Bharat Muni. It shows that after the departure of Indra court musicians, the common musician could not have sung two notes higher i.e. on Gandhar. So Bharat might have assumed that Gandhar Gram was not useful for Mrit Loka musicians and hence prohibited. The Madhyam Gram was accepted for female musicians.

Grams

The congregation of dependent notes is called Gram. Grams are of two types :

(a) Shadaja Gram.

(b) Madhyam Gram.

Pancham when fixed on fourth Shruti is called Shadaj Gram and when fixed on Third Shruti, it is called Madhyam Gram i.e. Dhaivat in Shadaja Gram is of three Shrutis and in Madhyam Gram is of four Shrutis.

If Gandhar be fixed on one Shruti each of Rishabha and Madhyam, Dhaivat on the Shruti of Panchama and Nishada on the Shruti of Dhaivata and Shadaja, it is called Gandhar Gram. It is expressed by Muni Narad. This Gram is popular in heaven and not on earth.

Shadaja is the starter and the key note. It has several Samvadi (Harmonic) notes. The medium note is not omitted in Odava and Shadava. Gandhar due to origin in Deva Loka is considered as key note. Hence only three notes—Shadaja, Madhyam and Gandhar are taken as Grams.

Shadaja gram = 4 Sa 3 Re 2 Ga 4 Ma 4 Pa 3 Dha 2 Nee = 22

Madhyam gram = 4M 3P 4Dha 2Nee 4Sa 3Re 2Ga = 22
              4S 3Re 4G 2Ma 4Pa 3Dha 2Nee = 22

Gandhar gram = 2Ga 4Ma 4Pa 3Dha 2Nee 4Sa 3Re = 22
               2Sa 4Re 4G 3M 2Pa 4Dha 3Nee = 22

Shadaj Gram Murchhana

The first Murchhana 'utara mandra' of Shadaja Gram, starts from Shadaja and the rest of Murchhanas start from nishada located in Mandra Sthana (lower Octave) *Madhyam gram Murchhana* : The first sauvery Murchhana of Madhyam Gram starts from Madhyam located in the Middle of Shadaja gram, and other six Murchhanas start from Gandhar.

Bharat Muni has explained Gram and Murchhanas without distorted notes and frets on Veena. Every musician had to tune his veena according to his voice.

Bharat Muni has pictured two numbers of Veena resembling one another in size and number of strings containing 22 strings on each for shrutis. The string of the first Shruti being tuned on the basis of the throat voice of the musician and after that strings of other Shrutis be turned in ascending order step by step upward showing double sound on the first Shruti of the upper octave. In this way both the Veenas should be tuned equally and gone of them kept as Achal or fixed Veena. The second chal or movable Veena for fixing notes on it. But for fixing the Notes for Murchhanas on the chal or movable Veena 22 more strings for lower octave shrutis are needed. In this way the movable (chal Veena) should have at least 22+22=44 strings.

Bharat has suggested that Madhyam Gram be started from Ma of Shadaja Gram and has also suggested Pa note to lower down one Shruti to provide Re note of Madhyam Gram as the Ma note of Shadaja Gram would become Sa note and provision be made for Re of three shrutis.

The following points should be kept in mind about Grams :

1. There was no fixed tone for Sa note at that time like that 'C' middle, fixed by the foreign musicians of to-day.

2. Frets were not fixed at Veena at that time.

3. Besides Shuddha Swaras (Natural notes) no Komal, (Half tone) or sharp note (Tivra Swara) was fixed in Grams.

4. The Veenas of Shadaja and Madhyam Grams were separate i.e. Veena of Shadaja Gram of Sa note was fixed on the 4th Shruti and Veena of Madhyam Gram at Ma note (Sa) was fixed on 13th Shruti. The Veenas at that time were not played like the Sitar of today. The strings were struck by the fingers or some small wooden or iron patti or blade.

Such a Veena seems to resemble with Swar Mandal and the method of playing might be based on it.

The views of Bharat show that the Grams were made on the basis of throat voice or pitch and the basic notes were used in every Gram. The Sa note was fixed and named Shadaja Gram on the basis of pitch.

Gram and Murchhanas are separate things. Even Gram fixes the position of note of natural note while Murchhana fixes the distorted note at different notes on shrutis as there were no Komal Half tone or Tivra Swaras Sharp notes at that time. They were made by changing the positions of notes called Murchhanas every shruti could become so for Murchhanas but not for any Grams. The Veenas of Shadaja and Madhyam Grams were based on the pitch and hence were separate.

We have shown the three Grams based on throat voice through charts :

Shadaja Gram—4 Sa 3 Re 2 Ga 4 Ma 4 Pa 3 Dha 2 Nee
With No. of shrutis :

Madhyam Gram—4 Sa 3 Re 2 Ga 4 Ma 4 Pa 3 Dha 2 Nee
With No. of shrutis :

Gandhar Gram—4 Sa 3 Re 2 Ga 4 Ma 4 Pa 3 Dha 2 Nee
With No. of shrutis.

Note.—The above three Grams can be fixed on Shruti No. 4 on the basis of throat voice on separate Veenas. It seems that they were sung on 4 or 7 srtinged Veenas tuned according to Grams and Murchhanas on 22 strings Veena. We have fixed Murchhanas on 44 strings as explained by Bharata and then further fixed them on 22 strings. In this way every Murchhana can be fixed on shrutis of Shadaja Gram—and every Murchhana maintains its own scale.

The Grams and Murchhanas of Shadaja and Madhyam Grams should be separate, hence shown separately.

Shadaja Gram Murchhanas

1.	Uttramandra	=	4 Sa	3 Re	2 Ga	4 Ma	4 Pa	3 Dha	2 Nee	
2.	Rajni	=	2 Nee	4 Sa	3 Re	2 Ga	4 Ma	4 Pa	3 Dha	
3.	Shudh Shadaja	=	3 Dha	2 Nee	4 Sa	3 Re	2 Ga	4 Ma	4 Pa	
4.	Mataszi	=	4 Pa	3 Dha	2 Nee	4 Sa	3 Re	2 Ga	4 Ma	
5.	Mulankirta	=	4 Ma	4 Pa	3 Dha	2 Nee	4 Sa	3 Re	2 Ga	
6.	Ashav Kranta	=	2 Ga	4 Ma	4 Pa	3 Dha	2 Nee	4 Sa	3 Re	
7.	Abhindgatta	=	3 Re	2 Ga	4 Ma	4 Pa	3 Dha	2 Nee	4 Sa	

Madhyam Gram Murchhanas

1.	Shudh Madhyam	=	4 Sa	3 Re	2 Ga	4 Ma	4 Pa	3 Dha	2 Nee	
2.	Margi	=	2 Nee	4 Sa	3 Re	2 Ga	4 Ma	4 Pa	3 Dha	2 Nee
3.	Pauravi	=	3 Dha	2 Nee	4 Sa	3 Re	2 Ga	4 Ma	4 Pa	
4.	Hirashyaka	=	4 Pa	3 Dha	2 Nee	4 Sa	3 Re	2 Ga	4 Ma	
5.	Savery	=	4 Ma	4 Pa	3 Dha	2 Nee	4 Sa	3 Re	2 Ga	
6.	Hari Ashva	=	2 Ga	4 Ma	4 Pa	3 Dha	2 Nee	4 Sa	3 Re	
7.	Kalopanta	=	3 Re	2 Ga	4 Ma	4 Pa	3 Dha	2 Nee	4 Sa	

Gandhar Gram Murchhanas

1.	Sumukhi	=	3 Sa	2 Re	4 Ga	3 Ma	3 Pa	3 Dha	4 Nee
2.	Chitra	=	4 Nee	3 Sa	2 Re	4 Ga	2 Ma	3 Pa	3 Dha

3. Chitravati	=	3 Dha	4 Nee	3 Sa	2 Re	4 Ga	3 Ma	3 Pa
4. Sukha	=	3 Pa	3 Dha	4 Nee	3 Sa	2 Re	4 Ga	3 Ma
5. Alapi	=	3 Ma	3 Pa	3 Dha	4 Nee	3 Sa	2 Re	4 Ga
6. Nanda	=	4 Ga	3 Ma	3 Pa	3 Dha	4 Nee	3 Sa	2 Re
7. Vishala	=	2 Re	4 Ga	3 Ma	3 Pa	3 Dha	4 Nee	3 Sa

Time Chart of Grams

Gram	God	Time of Singing	
		Season	Period
Shadaj	Brahmma	Hemant	Forenoon
Madhyam	Visnu	Summer	Noon
Gandhar	Mahesh	Rainy	After-noon

(6—8)

Murchanna

The systematic ascent and descent of seven notes is called the Murchhana. The above Murchhanas are of four types of each Shuddha, Kaklinished, Santra, Antarkakli, i.e. 14 × 14=56 in all.

Jatis of Murchhana

1.	Shuddha	4 Ma	3 Pa	4 Dha	2 Nee	4 Sa	3 Re	2 Ga
2.	Kaklikahila	4 Ma	3 Pa	4 Dha	2 Nee	4 Sa	3 Re	2 Ga
3.	Santara	2 Ma	3 Pa	4 Dha	2 Nee	4 Sa	3 Re	4 Ga
4.	Tadadvayoveta	2 Ma	3 Pa	4 Dha	4 Nee	2 Sa	3 Re	4 Ga

In the medieval period of Gram Murchhana system little by little became weak and the musicians began to adopt the Thata system. Now a days the Thata system is popular in whole of India.

	Shadaj Gram	Madhyam Gram
	Start from Shruti No. 4	Start from Shruti No. 13

Shruti	Shadaj Gram	Madhyam Gram
7	R	R
8		
9	G G	G G
10		
11		
12		
13	M M M	M M M
14		
15		
16		
17	P P P P	P P P P
18		
19		
20	D D D D D	D D D D D
21		
22	N N N N N N	N N N N N
1		
2		
3		
4	S S S S S S S S	S S S S S S S
5		
6		
7	R R R R R R R	R R R R R R
8		
9	G G G G G G	G G G G G G
10		
11		
12		
13	M M M M M	M M M M M
14		
15		
16		
17	P P P P	P P P P
18		
19		
20	D D D	D D D
21		
22	N N	N N

Shadaj Gram

1								
2			N					G
3				D				R
4	S	S			P	M		
5				N				G
6			S				M	
7	R	R			D			
8						P		
9	G	G	R	S	N			M
10							P	
11			G			D		
12				R				
13	M	M			S	N	D	P
14				G				
15			M				N	
16					R			D
17	P	P				S		
18				M	G			N
19			P				S	
20	D	D				R		
21								
22	N	N	D	P	M	G	R	S
No	1	2	3	4	5	6	7	

Madhyam Gram

1								
2			N					G
3				D				R
4	S	S			P	M		
5				N				G
6			S				M	
7	R	R			D			
8						P		
9	G	G	R	S	N			M
10							P	
11			G			D		
12				R				
13	M	M			S	N	D	P
14				G				
15			M				N	
16					R			D
17	P	P				S		
18				M	G			N
19			P				S	
20	D	D				R		
21								
22	N	N	D	P	M	G	R	S
No	1	2	3	4	5	6	7	

13

Thatas

The Indian music ran under a change since eleventh century A.D. It came under the influence of Iranian system of music which defused the old Indian system of music. Rag-Ragini system was popular in whole of India at that time. The scale system has first of all been described in Rag Tarangini written by poet Lochan. This book was written in the beginning of 15th century. The poet Lochan in this book has described the Thatas (scales) in place of Gram Murchhanas and has drawn out Ragas from 12 Thatas. He has supposed his natural Thata according to Kafee Thata of today. The authors of the books after Rag Tarangini have mentioned the Thata system.

The Twelve Thatas of Rag Tarangini

1. Bhairavi
2. Tordi
3. Gauri
4. Karshat
5. Kedar
6. Yaman
7. Sarang
8. Megh
9. Dhanashri
10. Purvi
11. Mukhari
12. Deepak

In 17th century A.D. Pt. Viyankat Mukhee wrote 1 the 'Chatur Dandika Prakashika'. He postulated 72 Thatas out of 12 notes (natural, half tone and sharp note of Octave). According to Viyankat Mukhee the 12 notes of Octave cannot be more than 72 Thatas. Nowadays only 12 Thatas are popular in South music.

The books were written on the system of scales but the musicians did not adopt them. Little by little the system came into practice. In seventh century Bhava Bhat wrote three books on music ;

1. Ashva Sangeet Ratnakar.
2. Anoop Vilas
3. Anoop Ankush Anoop.

In Ashva Sangeet Ratnakara he has adopted 20 scales for representing Ragas. He adopted Mukhari as his main scale. In the beginning of 19th century Mohammed Raza of Patna wrote a book Nagmate Asafee on music. He classified all the notes from the very base supposing Bilaval Thata as Natural Thata and discarded Rag-Ragini system.

In 20th century Pt. Vishnu Narayan Bhatkhande laid foundation of the Northern music system supposing Bilaval Thata as natural scale. He absorbed the 72 scales of Viyankat Mukhee in his 10 Thatas. This system is most popular in Northern India to-day.

Thatas

Thatas have borne out of 12 notes of Octave i.e. Thata is the combination of any seven notes of the Octave. Thatas are a kind of change of scale through which Ragas and Raginis are sung and played. Just as through the chain of Ragas of Kalyan Thata one sings Bhupali, Kedara and Hamir Ragas.

Points to Remember about Thatas

1. We cannot have a Thata of less than seven notes because if we have the Thata of less than seven notes then the Ragas having seven notes will not be sung through it.

2. The notes of Thata should be arranged serially as Sa, Re, Ga, Ma, Pa, Dha, Nee. By disturbing this arrangement the Thata will not take its true shape.

3. The chain of notes of Thata is uniform in ascent and descent. Hence, ascent and descent are not essential in a Thata because the notes of Thata already remain arranged in order—Sa Re Ga Ma Pa Dha Nee. The arrangement of notes remains uniform towards ascent and descent whatever is the nature of notes full tone, half tone or sharp notes. The notes are arranged in Sa Re Ga Ma Pa Dha

4. Nee order. The Thata can be recognised by the sound. Full tone, half tone or sharp tone etc. as—S R G M P D N. Ga, Dha and Nee in this Thata are half tone and all other are full tone notes. This combination of notes gives an idea of Asavari Raga.

   Thata is not the matter of singing. It is a combination of notes which is essentially pronounced, hence cannot produce attraction to the audience.

5. To recognize the Thatas the prominent name of that combination is demarcated such as Kalyan Thata—S R G Ḿ P D N. Now this Thata will be distinguished by the prominent name of this combination of Kalyan Raga. Kalyan Raga also called the That Vachak Raga.

6. On the basis of Indian System of Music i.e. according to the views of Bhatkhande both the types of note cannot be used in Thata.

Thata is a medium of knowledge of notes. It cannot be improvised or sung.

Method of Formation of Thata

Thata is formed by combining together any seven out of twelve notes of Octaves whether natural or distorted. At the time of formation of notes one should remember that notes should be arranged in a regular manner.

First of all we shall form Thata in which both type of notes are not used. If Sa of upper Octave is combined with S R G M P D N S notes of octave it makes eight notes of an Octave i.e. S R G M P D N S. Now we are giving the method of formation of different shapes of 8 notes. 'M' sharp will not be used in these 8 notes. They will be 16 in number. If 'Ma' sharp is used in place of Ma natural it makes 16 Thatas of that kind i.e. it makes 32 Thatas of that type.

For example according to Indian System 32 Thatas are made out of natural and distorted notes. If both the forms of notes are used with them, they become 72 in numbers.

Based on Indian System

1. S R G M   P D N S
2. S R G M   P D N S
3. S R G M   P D N S
4. S R G M   P D N S

Based on Karnatakee System

1. S R G M   P D N S
2. S R G M   P D N S
3. S R G M   P D N S
4. S R G M   P D N S
5. S R R M   P D N S
6. S G G M   P D N S

If 4 forms of Indian System are made together with P D N S of second side, they become 4×4=16. These are the 16 forms of Ma natural. If Ma sharp is used instead of Ma natural it will increase 16 more i.e. 16+16=32.

Thatas of M Natural

1. S R G M   P D N S   Bilaval Thata
2. S R G M   P D N S
3. S R G M   P D N S
4. S R G M   P D N S
5. S R G M   P D N S
6. S R G M   P D N S   Bhairava Thata
7. S R G M   P D N S
8. S R G M   P D N S
9. S R G M   P D N S   Khamaj Thata
10. S R G M   P D N S
11. S R G M   P D N S   Kafee Thata
12. S R G M   P D N S
13. S R G M   P D N S
14. S R G M   P D N S

90

15. S R G M   P D N S   Asavari Thata

16. S R G M   P D N S   Bhairavi Thata

Thatas of M Sharp

17. S R G Ḿ   P D N S   Kalyan Thata

18. S R G Ḿ   P D N S   Bhairva Thata

19. S R G Ḿ   P D N S

20. S R G Ḿ   P D N S

21. S R G Ḿ   P D N S

22. S R G Ḿ   P D N S   Purvi Thata

23. S R G Ḿ   P D N S

24. S R G Ḿ   P D N S

25. S R G Ḿ   P D N S

26. S R G Ḿ   P D N S

27. S R G Ḿ   P D N S   Todi Thata

28. S R G Ḿ   P D N S

29. S R G Ḿ   P D N S

30. S R G Ḿ   P D N S

31. S R G Ḿ   P D N S

32. S R G Ḿ   P D N S

Out of these 32 Thatas 10 are accepted by Bhatkhande. These 10 Thatas are 1—6—9—11—15—16—17—18—22 and 26 th.

Ten Thatas of Indian System

1. *Bilaval Thata*—All the notes in this Thata are natural Sa, Re, Ga, Ma, Pa, Dha, Nee, Sa.

2. *Kalyan Thata*—In this Thata Ma is the sharp note and all others are natural notes—Sa, Re, Ga, Ḿa Pa Dha Nee Sa.

3. *Khamaj Thata*—In [this Thata *Nee* is of half tone and all the rest are natural notes—Sa, Re, Ga, Ma, Pa, Dha, *Nee* Sa.

4. *Bhairava Thata*—In this Thata *Re* and *Dha* are half tone notes and all the rest are natural notes—Sa *Re* Ga Ma Pa *Dha* Nee Sa.

5. *Kafee Thata*—In this Thata *Ga,* and *Nee* half tone notes and all the rest are natural notes—Sa, Re, *Ga*, Ma, Pa, Dha, *Nee,* Sa.

6. *Asavary Thata*—In this Thata *Ga, Dha* and *Nee* half tone notes and all the rest are natural notes—Sa Re Ga Ma Pa Dha Nee Sa.

7. *Bhairavi Thata*—In this Thata *Re Ga Dha* and *Nee* half tone notes and all the rest are natural—Sa *Re Ga* Ma Pa *Dha Nee* Sa.

8. *Todi Thata*—In this Thata *Re Ga Dha* half tone and Ḿa sharp and all the rest are natural notes—Sa *Re Ga* Ma Pa Dha Nee Sa

9. *Marva Thata*—In this Thata *Re* half tone-Ḿa sharp note and all others are full tone notes—Sa, *Re* Ga Ḿa Pa Dha Nee Sa.

10. *Purvi Thata*—In this Thata *Re* and *Dha* half tone and Ma sharp note and the rest are natural notes Sa *Re* Ga Ḿa Pa *Dha* Nee Sa.

According to Pt. Viyankat Mukhee 72 Thatas are born out of natural and distorted notes of Octave. Before understanding the method of origin of these 72 Thatas, the knowledge of natural and distorted notes is essential.

Notes of Northern System	Notes of Southern System (according to Viyankat Mukhee)
1. Sa Fixed	Sa Fixed
2. Re Halftone	Re Natural
3. Re Natural	Re Panchshruti or Ga Natural
4. Ga Halftone	Re Shatshruti or Ga simple
5. Ga Natural	Ga Antra
6. Ma Natural	Ma Natural
7. Ma Sharp	Ma Prati or Ma Varahi

8. Pa Fixed	Pa Fixed
9. Dha Halftone	Dha Natural
10. Dha Natural	Dha Panchshruti or Nee Natural
11. Nee Halftone	Dha Shatshruti or Nee Kaishki
12. Nee Natural	Nee Kaklee.

Pt. Viyankat Mukhee put forth some rules to form 72 Thatas. They are as follows :—

1. Sa, Ma and Pa will be the same.

2. Panchshruti Re will be called Ga natural where natural Re and Panchshruti Re come together.

3. If Shatshruti Re comes together with Panchshruti Re. It will be called Ga simple.

4. If Ga simple comes at the place of Ga Antar, it will be called Shatshruti Re and in place of Ga natural it will be called Panchshruti Re.

5. If Panchshruti Dha comes together with Natural Dha it will be called only Panch-shruti Nee.

6. If Shatshruti Dha comes together with Panchshruti Dha and Natural Dha it will be Kaishki Nee.

7. If Kaishki Nee and Natural Nee come together with Kaishki Nee they will be called the Panchshruti Dha and Shatshruti Dha.

By the above rules we should conclude that both types of the same notes should be placed in an Octave together and they should be given any name.

The first four forms of Karnatakee system are the same as of Indian system but in 5th and 6th both the forms of notes are used together. For example in No. 5 Re halftone and Re natural have been used together and Ga natural has been omitted. In No. 6 Ga halftone and Ga natural have been used together and Re has been omitted. So these six forms are of one side. If P D N and S forms are combined with them, they will make $6 \times 6 = 36$. They are the 36 Thatas of Ma natural. If Ma sharp is used instead of Ma natural they make 36 Thatas more to make further $36 + 36 = 72$.

72 Thatas of Pt. Viyankat Mukhee

36 Thatas of M Natural		36 Thatas of M Sharp	
1. S R G M	P D N S	1. S R G Ḿ	P D N S
2. S R G M	P D N S	2. S R G Ḿ	P D N S
3. S R G M	P D N S	3. S R G Ḿ	P D N S
4. S R G M	P D N S	4. S R G Ḿ	P D N S
5. S R R M	P D N S	5. S R R Ḿ	P D N S

93

#									#								
6.	S	G	G	M	P	D	N	S	6.	S	G	G	M	P	D	N	S
7.	S	R	G	M	P	D	N	S	7.	S	R	G	Ḿ	P	D	N	S
8.	S	R	G	M	P	D	N	S	8.	S	R	G	Ḿ	P	D	N	S
9.	S	R	G	M	P	D	N	S	9.	S	R	G	Ḿ	P	D	N	S
10.	S	R	G	M	P	D	N	S	10.	S	R	G	Ḿ	P	D	N	S
11.	S	R	R	S	P	D	N	S	11.	S	R	R	Ḿ	P	D	N	S
12.	S	G	G	M	P	D	N	S	12.	S	G	G	Ḿ	P	D	N	S
13.	S	R	G	M	P	D	N	S	13.	S	R	G	Ḿ	P	N	D	S
14.	S	R	G	M	P	D	N	S	14.	S	R	G	Ḿ	P	D	N	S
15.	S	R	G	M	P	D	N	S	15.	S	R	G	Ḿ	P	D	N	S
16.	S	R	G	M	P	D	N	S	16.	S	R	G	Ḿ	P	D	N	S
17.	S	R	R	M	P	D	N	S	17.	S	R	R	Ḿ	P	D	N	S
18.	S	G	G	M	P	D	N	S	18.	S	G	G	Ḿ	P	D	N	S
19.	S	R	G	M	P	D	N	S	19.	S	R	G	Ḿ	P	D	N	S
20.	S	R	G	M	P	D	N	S	20.	S	R	G	Ḿ	P	D	N	S
21.	S	R	G	M	P	D	N	S	21.	S	R	G	Ḿ	P	D	N	S
22.	S	R	G	M	P	D	N	S	22.	S	R	G	Ḿ	P	D	N	S
23.	Ś	R	R	M	P	D	N	S	23.	S	R	R	Ḿ	P	D	N	S

24.	S $\underline{G}$ G M	P $\underline{D}$ $\underline{N}$ S
25.	S $\underline{R}$ G M	P $\underline{D}$ D S
26.	S $\underline{R}$ G M	P $\underline{D}$ D S
27.	S R $\underline{G}$ M	P $\underline{D}$ D S
28.	S $\underline{R}$ $\underline{G}$ M	P $\underline{D}$ D S
29.	S $\underline{R}$ R M	P $\underline{D}$ D S
30.	S $\underline{G}$ G M	P $\underline{D}$ D S
31.	S R G M	P N $\underline{N}$ S
32.	S $\underline{R}$ G M	P N $\underline{N}$ S
33.	S R $\underline{G}$ M	P N $\underline{N}$ S
34.	S $\underline{R}$ $\underline{G}$ M	P N $\underline{N}$ S
35.	S $\underline{R}$ R M	P N $\underline{N}$ S
36.	S $\underline{G}$ G M	P N $\underline{N}$ S

24.	S $\underline{G}$ G $\acute{M}$	P $\underline{D}$ $\underline{N}$ S
25.	S R G $\acute{M}$	P $\underline{D}$ D S
26.	S $\underline{R}$ G $\acute{M}$	P $\underline{D}$ D S
27.	S R $\underline{G}$ $\acute{M}$	P $\underline{D}$ D S
28.	S $\underline{R}$ $\underline{G}$ $\acute{M}$	P $\underline{D}$ D S
29.	S $\underline{R}$ R $\acute{M}$	P $\underline{D}$ D S
30.	S $\underline{G}$ G $\acute{M}$	P D $\underline{D}$ S
31.	S R G $\acute{M}$	P $\underline{N}$ N S
32.	S $\underline{R}$ G $\acute{M}$	P $\underline{N}$ N S
33.	S R $\underline{G}$ $\acute{M}$	P $\underline{N}$ N S
34.	S $\underline{R}$ $\underline{G}$ $\acute{M}$	P $\underline{N}$ N S
35.	S $\underline{R}$ R $\acute{M}$	P $\underline{N}$ N S
36.	S $\underline{G}$ G $\acute{M}$	P $\underline{N}$ N S

36 Thatas of Natural Medium Bhramari

1. Kankambari
2. Fenadyuti
3. Sam Barali
4. Bhanumati
5. Manoranjani
6. Tanukirati
7. Senagrani
8. Todi
9. Bhimshadaj
10. Natmabhran
11. Kokilkh
12. Roopavali
13. Hejujee
14. Basant Bhairavi
15. Malava Gaul
16. Veg Vahini
17. Chhayavati
18. Shuddha Malvi

19. Jhankar Bharmari	28. Kedar Gaul
20. Reeti Gaul	29. Shankar Bharan
21. Kiran Vali	30. Naga Bharan
22. Sri Rag	31. Kalavati
23. Gauri Belaval	32. Chudamani
24. Veer Vasant	33. Ganga Tarangini
25. Sharavati	34. Chhaya Natah
26. Tarangini	35. Deshakshi
27. Saur Sena	36. Chalnath

36 Thatas of Sharp Medium

37. Saugandhini	55. Shamla
38. Jaganmoheni	56. Chamra
39. Varalika	57. Somadyuti
40. Nabhomani	58. Singhravah
41. Kubhini	59. Dhamvati
42. Ravi Kiriya	60. Naishadah
43. Geervani	61. Kuntalh
44. Bhavani	62. Ratipriyah
45. Shevapantu Varali	63. Geetpriyah
46. Stavarajah	64. Bhushavati
47. Sauveera	65. Shantkalyan
48. Jeevantika	66. Chaturangini
49. Dhavalang	67. Santan Manjari
50. Namdeshi	68. Jiyoti
51. Ram Kriya	69. Dhaut Panchamah
52. Rama Manohari	70. Nasamani
53. Gamak Kriya	71. Kusumakar
54. Vansh Vati	72. Rasmanjari

14

Evolution of Ragas

Jati Gayan

Jati Gayan was popular in India in old times before the period of Sharang Deva. It has also been described by Bharat Muni in his Natya Shastra. He has explained it as a kind of tune sung in musical rhythm. Bharat Muni tried to accumulate all the tunes sung and played in various parts of the country and made common rules for singing and playing the Jati Gayan.

The word Raga was first of all used by Matang Muni in his book *Brahaddeshi* written in 6th Century A.D. 18 Jatis.

1. Madhya Modichya
2. Nandayanti
3. Ganadhar Panchami
4. Dhaivati.
5. Panchami.
6. Gandharo Dichyava
7. Arshibhi.
8. Nishadi.
9. Shadaj Kechaki
10. Shadajo dischayavati
11. Karmarvi
12. Andhari
13. Madhyama
14. Gandhari
15. Rakta Gandhari
16. Shadajee
17. Kechiki
18. Shadaj Madhyama

Two grams were popular at that time for Vocal and Instrumental Music for Jati Gayan.

(a) Shadaj Grama.

(b) Madhyam Grama.

These two gramas contained fourteen Murchhanas and the above 18 Jatis were sung and played on these two gramas.

The Lakshanas (characteristics) for the Jati Gayan have also been explained in Bharat Natya Shastra i.e. the Jati Gayan was practised according to these characteristics of Jatis.

97

The characteristics of Lakshanas are as follows :—

1.	Griha.	7.	Sanyasa
2.	Ansha	8.	Vinyasa
3.	Mandra	9.	Bahutatva
4.	Tara	10.	Alaptva
5.	Niyasa	11.	Shadavatva
6.	Upjiyas	12.	Odavatva

Grih : Greh is the note from where the singing and playing starts.

Ansha : It is the main note of the Raga and is used more than any other note of the Raga.

Mandira : Mandra tells the approach of Raga to a particular note of Lower Octave.

Tara : Tara denotes the approach of Raga to a particular note in Upper Octave.

Niyasa : The note on which the Raga ends, is called the Niyasa.

Upniyasa : The ending note of Prabandha, Vastu, Roopak Gayan etc. was called the Upniyasa.

Sanyasa : Sanyasa note is one on which the first part or the first line of the song, ends.

Vinyasa : Vinyasa is the note on which the first part of a particular tune ends.

Bahutatva : The use of repeatedly note in a Raga is called the Bahutva.

Alpatva : The use of note in light way in a Raga is called Alpatva. It is of two types :—

(a) Langhan and Alanghan.

(b) Abhyas and Anabhyas.

Langhan : The not which is omitted in Gayan is called *Langhan.*

Alanghan : The note which is not omitted in ascent and descent is called Alanghan This note is not omitted in any Jati Gayan. The not which is omitted in ascent or descent *Abhiyas.*

Anabhiyasa : Anabhyasa is the use of a Disconent note to increase the beauty of Raga.

Shadavatva : Shadavatva shows the number of notes. The Ragas in which six notes are in ascent and descent is called Shadavatva.

Odavatva : The Ragas in which the five number of notes are used in their ascent and descent is called Odavatva.

These Lakshanas show that the old Jati Gayans were sung in the same manner as the Ragas of today.

In time of Sarang Deva Nibaddha and Anibaddha Gayans came in practice and Prabandha, Vastu and Roopakas etc., were also sung. The Prabandha Gayan of old days very much resembled with Dhrupad Gayan of today and the old Prabandha Gayan was categorised in many parts. These parts were known as Udgriha, Milapa, Dhruva, Antra and

Abhoga. They were also called Dhatu. Besides Prabandha, Vastu and Roopak there was another Gayan popular in those days and it was Alapatika. This Gayan was used to express the features of Raga.

Sharang Deva in his Sangeet Ratnakara, has divided the music of those days in two parts. These parts are called Nibadha and Anibadha.

Nibaddha Gayan : The time and rhythmical geets containing Ugdreha, Milapa Dhruva, Antra and Abhoga etc. were called the Nibaddha Gayans.

Anibaddha Gayan : The Gayan which is not controlled by time and rhythm and the features of the song can be recognised by the prolongation of notes is called the Anibaddha Gayan (Alapa).

When Rag-Ragini system became popular these Lakshanas were accepted by the musical circle and the Rag-Rainis were sung and played on the basis of these Lakshanas.

There is difference of opinion about the names of Lakshnas. This can be seen in the following table :—

LAKSHAANS

Sharang Deva	*Viyankat Mukhee*
1. Girah	Girah
2. Ansha	Ansha
3. Mandra	Mandra
4. Tara	Tara
5. Niyasa	Niyasa
6. Upniyasa	Upniyasa
7. Alpatava	Sanyasa
8. Bahutatva	Vinyasa
9. Shadavatata	Bahutatva
10. Odavatatva	Alpatatva

15

Rag-Ragini System

After the formation of Jati Gayan the condition of Indian music was not improved due to foreign invasions. The Indian music fell into two divisions :—

(a)   Northern Indian music, called the Hindustan Sangeet system

(b)   Southern music, called the Karnataki Sangeet system

On account of effect of invasions the musical activities remained at standstill in North but music in South India stepped towards developments on the lines of old music system but the northern music due to alien contact of Arab countries and Persia started new Rag-Ragini system.

To understand the deep characteristics and the knowledge of new get up of Indian music one will have to admit that the alien music was already germinated on Indian style and basic principles. History admits that Indian musicians in 11th Century A.D. went to Arab countries and popularised Indian music there. When they invaded India they brought musicians with them. These musicians, though foreign in origin and nationality, might have surely been affected by the Indian musicians. It may also be possible that these musicians may belong to the descendants of those migrated to Arab countries from India. It may be assumed that they may have hereditary musical taste as is seen in families of different stages that the sons follow the professions of their fathers and so on. Music, which is assumed a an art, is related with human society and is not affected by the country, creed and religious bindings. Hence the musicians who came in India from abroad might have been surely familiar with our culture and civilization because expressing of Ragas by prolongation creating rasas in music and expression of inner feelings by musical rhythm is the work of Indian music only. On account of this fact we consider that Rag-Ragini system is the mixture of Indian and alien music.

Before the begining of Thata System Rag-Ragini was popular in whole of India and the classification of Ragas was done in form of a family member. There were six main Ragas according to this system. Every Raga had five Raginis, Eight Sons and Son's wives each thus making 6 Ragas' $6 \times 5 = 30$ Raginis, $6 \times 8 = 48$ Sons, and the same number i.e 48 of Son's wives to form 132 Raga-Raginis in all. Every opinion or the doctrine differed to confirm the names of Rag-Raginis. There were four main matas or schools (groups) about the above discussions.

1 Kalinath Mata's Group
2 Shameshwar Mata's Group
3 Hanuman Mata's Group
4 Bharat Mata's Group

Kalinath   *Shameshwar*

Hanuman   *Bharat*

Kalinath Mata

This mata started after the name of Sri Krishna. People say that Sri Krishna in his childhood was playing with a ball on the bank of river Jamuna with his Gwala friends. The ball by chance fell into the river. The child Krishna jumped into the river to get the ball out. In the river water lived a Sheshnaga (King of Snakes) having a thousand hoods. It pounced upon the child Krishna to bite him but Sri Krishna very smartly rode over the hoods of Sheshnaga and kept on dancing and playing flute on the hoods to save himself from biting. Whatever Ragas and Talas he improvised at that time, are known as Ragas of Kalinath Mata. The Ragas and Raginis according to this Mata are as follows :

Bhairava, Siri, Basant, Pancham, Nat Narayan and Megh.

1. **Bhairava Raga :—**

   (i) Bhairavi (ii) Gujari (iii) Reva (iv) Gunakalee (v) Bengali.

2. **Siri Raga :—**

   (i) Malvi (ii) Triveni (iii) Kedari (iv) Madhur Madhvi (v) Gauri.

3. **Basant Raga :—**

   (i) Deshi (ii) Devagiri (iii) Baradi (iv) Todi (v) Lalit.

4. **Pancham Raga :—**

   (i) Vibhas (ii) Bhoopali (iii) Patmanjari (iv) Malsri (v) Badhans.

5. **Nat Narayan Raga :—**

   (i) Kamodi (ii) Kalyani (iii) Sarang (iv) Nat Hamir (v) Natika.

6. **Megh Raga :—**

   (i) Malhari (ii) Sorathi (iii) Savery (iv) Kaushiki (v) Gandhari.

Shameshwar Mata

Shameshwar Mata is also called the Shiva or the Brahma Mata. It came into practice after the style of music played by Shiva-Parbati. The followers of this system accepted six main Ragas. These six Ragas were as follows :—

Bhairava, Siri, Basant, Pancham, Nat Narayan and Megha. Every Raga had five queens, eight sons and eight sons wives. There are Five Raginis of each Raga :

1. **Bhairava Raga :**

   (i) Bhairvi (ii) Gujari (iii) Reva (iv) Gunakari (v) Bengali.

2. **Sri Raga :**

   (i) Malva (ii) Gauri (iii) Kedara (iv) Madhu Madhvi (v) Pahari.

3. **Basant Raga :**

   (i) Deshi (ii) Devgiri (iii) Baradi (iv) Todi (v) Lalit.

4. **Pancham Raga :**

   (i) Vibhas (ii) Bhupali (iii) Budhans (iv) Malsari (v) Patmanjari.

5. **Nat Narayan Raga :**

   (i) Kamodi (ii) Kalyani (iii) Gauri (iv) Natika (v) Sarang.

6. **Megh Raga :**

   (i) Malhar (ii) Soratha (iii) Savery (iv) Gandhari (v) Kaushiki

Hanuman Mata

The originator of Hanuman Mata is supposed to be Hanuman, the devotee of Sri Rama. The style of songs which he sang in the devotion to Rama, became famous after his name as Hanuman Mata. The Ragas and Raginis of Hanuman Mata are as follows :

Bhairava, Malkauns, Deepak, Hindol, Siri & Megh Raga.

1. **Bhairava Raga :**

   (i) Madhyama Medhavi (ii) Bhairavi (iii) Bengali (iv) Baradi (v) Sindhavi.

2. **Malkauns Raga :**

   (i) Todi (ii) Khambavati (iii) Gauri (iv) Gunakali (v) Kukambhi.

3. **Deepak Raga :**

   (i) Kedara (ii) Kandra (iii) Deshi (iv) Kambodi (v) Nut.

4. **Hindol Raga :**

   (i) Bilavali (ii) Devashakha (iii) Lalit (iv) Patmanjari (v) Ramkali.

5. **Siri Raga :**

   (i) Basant (ii) Malvi (iii) Malsri (iv) Dhanasri (v) Asavari.

6. **Megh Raga :**

   (i) Malhar (ii) Deshkari (iii) Bhupali (iv) Gujari (v) Tank.

Bharat Mata

About the origin of Bharat Mata people hold two types of opinions. Some say that this Mata owes its origin to Bharat, the younger brother of Sri Rama. They say when Rama was exiled for 14 years by his father Dushratha, Bharata ruled over the kingdom of Ayodhya by placing Sandals of Rama on the throne as a symbol of his presence. In this period of 14 years whatever Bharat sang in devotion to his brother—Rama, was named as Bharat Mata after him.

According to the other opinion Bharat Mata took its origin after saint Bharat who wrote Bharat Natya Shastra. People who follow the second opinion accept Bhairava, Mulkauns, Deepak, Hindol, Siri & Megh Ragas and five Raginis of each :

1. **Bhairva Raga :**

   (i) Madhumaya (ii) Bhairavi (iii) Bengali (iv) Baradi (v) Sindhavi.

2. **Malkauns Raga :**

   (i) Todi (ii) Khambavati (iii) Gaudi (iv) Gunakali (v) Kukambha.

3. **Deepak Raga :**

   (i) Natmalhari (ii) Kandha (iii) Kedara (iv) Deshi (v) Pahari.

4. **Hindole Raga :**

   (i) Bilavali (ii) Ramkali (iii) Patmanjari (iv) Dev Shakhya (v) Lalit.

5. **Siri Raga :**

   (i) Basant (ii) Malvi (iii) Malsari (iv) Dhanasri (v) Asavari.

6. **Megh Raga :**

   (i) Malahari (ii) Deshkari (iii) Bhupali (iv) Bahusi (v) Gujari.

The Time Factor of the Old Ragas

Those who follow Raga—Ragini system, they fix the time of singing them according to the seasons. A particular Rag—Ragini was sung according to the seasonal taste. The main Raga was called the king of the season. In India we have six seasons of two months each. The detailed description of the above Ragas is given as follows :

Seasons	Shameshwar Mata	Bharat Mata	Kalinath Mata	Hanuman Mata
Spring	Pancham	Hindole	Pancham	Hindole
Summer	Nat Narayan	Deepak	Nat Narayan	Deepak
Rainy	Megh	Megh	Megh	Megh
Sharad	Bhairava	Bhairava	Bhairava	Bhairava
Hemant	Sri	Sri	Sri	Sri
Shishir	Basant	Malkauns	Basant	Malkauns

All the four Matas which have been described above were the four different schools which imparted education in music on their own style. It is an old convention in India that we people believe to name an institution, road or hospital after the name of forefathers. Hence on the same belief these four Matas also bore their names. The School of Hanuman Mata was more popular that time because a famous musician of Akbar's Court, Mian Tan Sen, represented that school. Tan Sen Ragas are still taken as Standard Ragas in Hindustani Music. 'Ragmala' of Gangadhar written in 1798 also took the ideas of Rag—Raginis from Hanuman Mata.

They have also given the true shape of Rag—Raginis with the help of clear pictures along with their effect on human life, are giving the sketches of Rag—Raginis according to Hanuman Mata. (Sharmai-Isharat).

The Ornamental Shape of Ragas

The ornamental shape of Rag-Raginis has been described with the historical introduction in Sangeet Darpana. Every Raga has been compared with human life. Following is the ornamental shape of six main Ragas and their Raginis according to Hanuman Mata.

Mahadeva, the god of music is distinguished by having five heads. Each of the four heads being turned towards the four quarters of the globe—North. South, East and West while the fifth head is turned towards the heaven and from each of the five great Ragas, originated Bhairava, Hindole, Deepak, Siri & Megha Ragas. The sixth Raga Malkauns comes out of Parbati, the wife of Mahadeva. Brahma created thirty Raginis.

Rag Bhairva	:	This great god tune originates that head of Mahadeva which is turned towards South.
Rag Siri	:	This great god tune originates that head of Mahadeva which is turned towards West.
Rag Malkauns	:	This great god tune originates from Parvati, the wife of Mahadeva.
Rag Hindole	:	This great god tune has sprung from that mouth of Mahadeva which is turned towards the North.
Rag Deepak	:	This great god tune of fire deeply is created out of that mouth of Mahadeva which is turned towards East.
Rag Megh	:	One of the six Raga god tune is the Lord of Rains. This has come out of the fifth head of Mahadeva which is turned towards heaven.

RAG BHAIRAVA

Rag Bhairava is compared with the sacred body of Lord Shiva representing Trishul in his hand, a garland of human skulls around his neck, snakes around his body, phases of moon on his forehead and river Ganges flowing out of his hair.

Bhairava Raga has five Raginis : 1. Madh-madhavi. 2. Baradi. 3. Bhairavi. 4. Bengal. 5. Sindhavi which are represented as ideal graces of womanhood, most divinely fair and of incomparable beauty. The radiance they shed is so great that it shames the sun, who hides his face behind the clouds and the moon withdraws in modest retirement on seeing their sweet lustre, a most prominent Ragini of above Raga is Bhairavi.

RAGINI BHAIRAVEEN, the goddess tune of Rag Bhairaon, is sylph-lime and most exquisitely proportioned. All the tender freshness and bloom of shy young maidenhood of fourteen years is her birthright. Her hair, still humid with the Shnan (sacred bath) is thrown back in a heavy dark mass. From beneath her long dropping eyelashes there escapes an ineffable light, giving a calm serenity to the beautiful profile. Her slim hands are clasped in reverence. Her whole attitude is being in submission of religious fervour, a breathing poem of devotion at the altar of "Linga". She has taken out her garland of heavily scented golden CHAMPA (flowers), and consecrated it to the gods. Her scheme of colour of costume and jewels is red and white. Her dainty person is bejewelled and enveloped in an opalescent gossamer of fairy imagination. The temple of MAHADEO is built on the summit of a hill encircled by a fort. Flowering blooms of the NEELOOFAR (blue lotus) scent the atmosphere. Two young maidens are engaged in playing and singing on the MAJERA (musical bells) and TAMBOURS. Pearly dawn is creeping invisibly, bathing the realm with a delicate, roseates light. This is the enchanted hour when the tune of BHAIRAVEEN is sung.

5 Raginis of Rag Bhairava

1. Madmadhavi 2. Baradi 3. Bhairavi 4. Bengal 5. Sindhavi

RAG SHIRI

Siri Raga is of eighteen years in age. In appearance it is like a man dressed in red garments, with a handsome pearl and ruby necklace and drops in the ears, a lotus flower in his hand, seated on a royal dais, absorbed in listening to the intoxicating strains of the

unrivalled BEEN (musical instrument), holding his lovely companion encased in a mystic lotus bloom, in his left hand, and in his right hand holding a naked sword; a monster fish (sign of royalty), stands upright in obedience to his commands. Siri Raga, famed all over the universe, sports sweetly with his nymphs, gathering fresh blossoms in the bosom of yon grove, and his Divine, lineaments are distinguished through his graceful vesture. Siri Rag has five Raginis: 1. Basant, 2. Malsari, 3. Dhanasri, 4. Asavari and 5. Marva. The Raginis, are represented as coy young maidens of surpassing loveliness, living in perpetual spring and seeking heavenly bliss in music.

RAGINI ASAVARI, the goddess tune of Rag Siri, has an ascetic character. It is represented as a female Jogi (one who has renounced the world), seated on a promontory inside a fort, surrounded towards her in tender protection and shading from the morning sun's warm rays. The hour for its performance is morning. Her dawning womanhood is arrayed in the simple salmon coloured garb of a Jogan, defining the beautiful and subtle lines of her figure. Her raven hair is massed on the top of the head in a Jata (sacred knot). On the white brow gleams the sacred mark of religion in camphor. Her slumbrous eyes are heavy and languorous with the power of her own music. Her sweet mouth is intent on blowing the soul stirring notes of the Pungi (musical instrument). Her personality glows with music. The deadly serpents and peacocks are attracted beyond control. They creep and crawl towards her fascinating being amazed and entranced, wholly worshipping her, coiling round her body with affection. The sandal wood tree has an affinity to serpents, so has the flute Pungi, which issues strange weird sounds, and so have the peacocks.

5. Raginis of Rag Shiri

1. Malsari, 2. Basant, 3. Asavari, 4. Dhanasari, 5. Marva

RAGA HINDOL

Hindol Raga is one whom the women are billing in a hindola having small strings and who is enjoying gay and happiness lustfully. People have described Raga hindol like this.

In form it is like Krishna, the god of love, squatting on a hindola, the mystic, golden swing, suspended in the ethereal regions by the Apsaras (celestial female singers), elegantly bejewelled, playing on the Bansri (magic flute), encircled by gaily dressed Gopis (maidens), who are swinging him in rhythm with the motion of the universe. The liquid depths of his eyes are brimful of mirth and love; locks dark as musk, are braided away from the forehead. Rainbow coloured draperies of gossamer airiness encircle the graceful forms of the young maidens, kissing the blooming cheeks and falling lightly over their heads. Jewels shed their brilliant lustre, enhancing the chiselled loveliness of face and figure. Hindol has five Raginis—Bilawal[2], Ramkali[1], Lalit[3], Deosakh[5] and Patmanjari[4]. The Raginis live in a nest of swansdown in their soft sweet thoughts. Their years of musical life roll smoothly by. Agility and power in a high degree are demanded in rendering the great Raga. There is a sequence of ascending and descending which flow with varied tone colours, changes in volume and speed, over a range of at least two and a half octaves, then dwelling upon the top note gradually returning to the original keytone without effort.

RAGINI LALIT, the goddess tune of Rag Hindol, is represented as the most brilliant specimen of feminine aristocracy. Her skin is lily-white alabaster with a lustrous glow behind it. Her bejewelled radiance and beautiful head poised on a graceful neck, defies rivalry of the jewelled arms, throat, ears and feet. Golden gauzes of scintillating tints of glorious colours and richness flout round her exquisite symmetrical form, disclosing the perfect lines. Her perfumed tresses are thrown in a dense cloud behind. The mysterious expression of her large limpid eyes is partly revealed in the shadow of the long dark, silken lashes which veil them. She reclines with ease on the flower besprinkled, gorgeous divan, subjugating the senses by her poetic grace and indefinable elegance. A woman with a garland of flowers is standing near her in attendance, gazing on her rapturously. A Been is lying idle nearby. The hindola (swing) sways to music.

5. Raginis of Rag Hindol

1. Ramkali, 2. Bilawal, 3. Lalit, 4. Patmanjari, 5. Deosakh

RAG MALKAUNS

Rag Malkauns is supposed to be of red bodied human being who has influenced heroes with his power to put on the garland of the enemies, and he has a red coloured garland around his neck. He is represented as a glorified image of the rich, deep, passionate, and mystical melody. Dressed in blue, his dreamy eyes are veiled with emotion. He is holding a severed human music by the maidens in the undefined distance. Towering on either side are the "Morechais" (insignia of royalty). In front crouches a poet singing his praises.

MALKAUNS has five Raginis—Khambavati[2]. Gunakali[1], Todi[3], Gouri[5] and Kukabh[4]. The Raginis are fair bevies of beauties, each lovelier than the other, dreaming away the warm hours of life in pleasant and sweet musings. No cares or trouble cross their serene paths; no clouds disturb the eternal gay sunshine of their lives. The idea of conquering enemies through the power of song is eternal in classical SANGEET. The Rags were qualified as brave undaunted warriors overcoming their formidable opponents with the mighty power of song. The great secret of a tone that is always steady, always pure, always true, is the art of breathing correctly. The breath taken should be inward and deep without physical effort, and not with the hitching up of the shoulders, audible aspirations, and breathiness in the sound. The breath is taken secretly, its volume so sustained that the singing will give an impression of exhaustless resources, like the rise and fall of pleasant winds. Like other classical Ragas, Malkauns has many sustained notes, hence the volume of sustained breath is important.

RAGINI TODI, the goddess tune of Rag Malkauns, is a highly classical extremely difficult melody. It is represented as a young maiden of ravishing beauty. Draped in white and gold, with the sacred mark of camphor and saffron on her brow, she stands on a hill top, resting gracefully on a willow tree, entwining a Sesame tree, wholly absorbed in playing on the Been, her pulse beats in rhythmic response to the swaying of the willowy foliage in a whirl of motion, causing the glowing crimson to mount the fair cheeks. The wild deer venture with in the sacred precincts in meek submission and adoration, completely subdued by so glorious a picture, and such thrilling music. Certain tunes attract certain animals in nature.

5. Raginis of Rag Malkauns

1. Gunkali, 2. Khambavati, 3. Todi, 4. Kukabh, 5. Gouri

113

RAG DEEPAK

One who blew out the lamp in playing and who was ashamed of the shining grandeur of his Ratnas (purples) is Rag Deepak to make a dark for a young lady.

This mystic Rag is extinct now and the legend attached to its extirpation is that the court musician, Tan Sen, was singing it in the presence of the mighty Emperor Akbar. His whole soul poured into the piece of music he was singing, and note after note vibrated through the air, and thrilled the element and the spellbound listeners. His song had no ending, till at last nature was moved beyond control. Fire was ignited through occult powers and the

place was in flames. This extraordinary incident has proved fatal to the tune and none has dared to sing it since. The awe and fear with which it is regarded even today is beyond belief. The greatest musician will bend his head in reverence and silence at the very name of Deepak and will refuse the honour of singing it. It is strange that an incident which happened centuries ago should still exercise the same influence on the minds of the people as if it had happened today. Deepak has five Raginis: (1) Desi, (2) Kamode, (3) Kandara, (4) Nut, and (5) Kedara. Kamode and Desi, are beauties in distress. Kedara is so lost in the thoughts of Mahadeo that she assumes his form Nut, and Kandara, are magificent women with moral and physical courage. "Daring and bold in war, ardent and impatient in love". Nut is represented as a conquering hero holding the severed head of the enemy in her hand.

RAGINI KANDARA, the goddess tune of Rag Deepak, is represented as a female warrior conqueror, with clear cut handsome features, standing straight, robed in white, and shimmering gems, a naked sword in one hand, and an elephant's tooth in the other hand. The entire premises is burning and dry with smouldering fire, a huge grey elephant is cowering before her supplicating for his lost tooth. Her delicate nostrils are dilating with disdain, and she gives him a withering glance. Her dark eyes flash fire. The time for its performance is early night. There are 18 varieties of Kandara.

5. Raginis of Rag Deepak
1. Desi, 2. Kamode, 3. Kandra, 4. Nut, 5. Kedara

RAG MEGH

Rag Megh is represented as a dark, handsome man of formidable appearance. He holds a naked sword in the hand flourishing it in mid air, as if to rend the very skies, growing and snarling in rage. He scowls heavily. His eyes are fierce. His hair is drawn upwards and twisted like a turban. The heavens are blackened with angry clouds. Thunder and lightening tear the murky, thick atmosphere, creating an altogether dreadful aspect. Megh was sung by Tan Sen, in the time of Emperor Akbar, and it brought forth torrents of rain, avoided famine, and cured pestilence. Megh is rendered in Gamak (glutral forceful variations), resembling thunder and storm, and only sung by strong powerful athletic exponents. Megh has five Raginis: (1) Malhar, (2) Bhoopali, (3) Gujari, (4) Deskar, and (5) Tunk. Bhopali is a bright most attractive and popular melody, and is Khadao (6 notes in the scale) and does not take ma, it originated in Bhopal (Bhopal), Malar is draped in white jesmine flowers, singing on the Dotara Tank, is also called Tilang, and much patronised in Punjab. She reclines on a diwan of lotus flowers. Deskar is represented as a beautiful female anointed with sandal wood paste, playing chess on a terrace.

RAGINI GOJRI, the goddess tune of Rag Megh, is represented floating on an island of water, with palaces of mists and bubbles of a hundred colours, made of lotus blooms. Fleecy clouds encircle her dainty limbs. She is seated on the foliage of lotus, playing and singing, accompanied by her lovely companions, existing in eternal bliss.

5 Raginis of Rag Megh
1. Malhar, 2. Bhopali, 3. Gujari, 4. Deskar, 5. Tunk

17

Sentiments

It is intended to describe the different sentiments or rasas and feelings recognised in the Indian rhetorics and poetry, and to explain briefly how they are produced or affected. The word feeling or the state of mind at any time is Bhava from the root to be, to exist. Distinction is made between a lasting feeling, or that which pervades the mind during the time under consideration, and those which are transitory, being excited by circumstances and then subsiding. The former is known as a *Sthai bhava* (enduring, permanent form to stand), the latter are called *Vyabhichari bhavas* (irregular and unfaithful).

The condition or circumstance which alter the existing one or excites a particular state of mind or body is called *Vibhava*. The sudden appearance of a poisonous snake, or some body's sudden calling out that there is a snake, which will generate the feeling of fear. It is Vibhava. Meeting or hearing about one's beloved or recollection of sweet old memories about him or her, which may excite feeling of love, is Vibhava. Vibhava is of two kinds—Alambana and Uddipana. The former (आलम्बन supporting) is that person or thing with reference to which a sentiment arises; the latter (उद्दीपन exciting) represents the causes which enhances its depth. In the case, for instance, of the feeling of sorrow over the death of somebody, the person dead is the Alambana of the sentiment, and the attending circumstances which aggravate sorrow are its Uddipana Vibhavas. Alambana or Uddipana may happen in three ways viz., Darshan i.e. by seeing; Shravana or by hearing; and Smarana or by recollection; as in the examples cited above.

When a feeling is excited in the mind, we usually find manifestation in some part of the body. The symptoms which thus indicate the feeling outwardly are called *Anubhavas*, pelpitation of the heart or drying of the mouth due to the feeling of fear is Anubhava. The pleasure expressed on the face of the lovers when they meet, and the sadness when they long to meet but cannot, are Anubhavas or the feeling of love.

The different feelings or bhavas excited by the appropriate Vibhavas and accompanied by their Anubhavas give rise to what are called Rasas. Rasas which means taste, essence or sentiment are a comprehensive term for an aggregate resultant emotion. *Rasaprabodha*, a Hindi

118

book written by S. Ghulam Nabi of Belgaon in 1741 A.D. describes Rasa in a very fine simile. It says, "The human mind is the soil where Rasa has got its seeds; *Sthaibhava* is the sprout which irrigated with the water of *Vibhava* grows into a plant called *Anubhava* according to the environments. *Vyabhicharibhavas* are the flowers, blossoming at frequent intervals and in consonance with the Sthai. These combined produce the honey called Rasa, which is collected by the poet acting as a bee".

The feelings which give rise to sentiments are grouped into nine as follows:—

1. *Rati* (रति)=pleasure, amusement, love, affection, sexual pleasure or passion;
2. *Hasya* (हास्य)=laughter, merriment, ridicule;
3. *Shoka* (शोक)=sorrow, grief, pitiableness;
4. *Krodha* (क्रोध)=anger, wrath;
5. *Utsaha* (उत्साह)=effort, determination, perseverance, firmness, fortitude;
6. *Bhaya* (भय)=fear, alarm, terror;
7. *Jugupsa* (जुगुप्सा)=censure, dislike, disgust;
8. *Vismaya* (विस्मय)—wonder, surprise, admiration; and
9. *Shanta* (शान्त)=tranquillity, rest, absence of passion, restraint of senses. The last has been put later on, because it is in fact absence of a real feeling. It has not been recognised by Bharata, the author of Natyashastra, as a feeling giving rise to a sentiment.

The Rasas which arise from the above feelings or bhavas are respectively known as :

1. *Shrangara* (शृंगार)
2. *Has* (हास्य)
3. *Karuna* (करुण) (sorrow)
4. *Raudra* (रौद्र) (wrathful, terrible)
5. *Vira* (वीर)
6. *Bhayanaka* (भयानक) (terror)
7. *Veebhatsa* (वीभत्स) (disgust)
8. Adbhuta (अद्भुत्) (marvellous); and
9. *Shanta* (शान्त) (undisturbed).

The last as said above is not recognised in the Natyashastra on the other hand, there are other writers who recognise two extra rasas—*Vatsalya* (वात्सल्य) or affection, especially for one's offspring, and *Bhakti* (भक्ति) or worship and devotion. These are surely included in Shrangara, Vira, Adbhuta, and Shanta.

Shrangara, the sentiment of love, is so called because it is the most important of the rasas (from Shringa peak of a mountain). It is also therefore known as Rasaraja. It is of two kinds, viz.

1. Sambhoga Shrangara, when the lovers enjoy each other's company, and
2. Vipralambha (विप्रलम्भा) Shrangara when there is separation due to any cause.

Vira (वीर), the sentiment of heroism is fourfold, viz.

119

A—*Dana Vira* (दानवीर) i.e., heroism based on liberality or the sentiment of enthusiastic liberality;

B—*Dharma Vira* (धर्म वीर) i.e., heroism based on piety and righteousness, or the sentiment of enthusiastic piety ;

C—*Daya Vira* (दयावीर) i.e., heroism based on compassion, or the sentiment of chivalrous compassion; and

D—*Yuddha Vira* (युद्धवीर) or heroism in battle.

No rather comments are needed in respect of the other rasas.

The nine bhavas noted above are Sthai when they are the pervading feelings of a particular Rasa, but when they come and go, strengthening the pervading feeling, they are *Vyabhichari*. The latter are known as :—

1—*Tanu Vyabhichari* when affecting the body and giving rise to Anubhavas, and

2—*Mana Vyabhichari* when affecting the mind.

The former manifests itself in eight ways, viz.

1—Sweda (स्वेद) sweating;

2—Stambha (स्तम्भ)—motionlessness;

3—Romancha (रोमांच)—horripilation or erection of hair;

4—Swara bhanga (स्वरभंग)—broken articulation;

5—Kampa (कम्प)—trembling;

6—Vivarna (विवर्ण)—change of colour;

7—Ashru (अश्रु)—tears; and

8—Pralapa (प्रलाप)—prattling, talking nonsense. Jrimbha (जृम्भा) or yawning is also included in this by some.

The latter (Mana Vyabhichari) has thirty-three manifestations viz.

1—Nirveda (निर्वेद)—indifference to worldly objects, self-humiliation;

2—Glani (ग्लानि)—exhaustion, fatigue;

3—Shanka (शंका)—fear, misgiving

4—Alasya (आलस्य)—want of energy;

5—Asuya (असूया)—envy, jealousy;

6—Shrama (श्रम)—exertion, weariness;

7—Mada (मद)—conceit;

8—Dainya (दैन्य)—miserable state, low spiritedness;

9—Chinta (चिन्ता)—anxiety;

10—Moha (मोह)—perplexity

11—Smriti (स्मृति)—recollection;

12—Dhriti (धृति)—contentment;

13—Vrida (व्रीडा)—Shame, bashfulness;

14—Harsha (हर्ष)—joy;

15—Chapalata (चपलता)—swiftness, fickleness, unsteadiness;

16—Jadata (जड़ता)—dullness;

17—Garva (गर्व)—Pride, arrogance;

18—Vishada (विषाद)—disappointment.

19—Avega (आवेग)—agitation, furry;

20—Utkantha (उत्कंठा)—longing for a beloved persons or thing;

21—Nidra (निद्रा)—sleepiness;

22—Swapna (स्वप्न)—dreaming;

23—Apasmara (अप्समार)—epilepsy (this manifests itself more as a tanu vyabhichari);

24—Avahittya (अवहित्या)concealment of an inward feeling;

25—Amarsha (अमर्ष)—anger due to disrespect etc., intolerance;

26—Ugrata (उग्रता)—ferociousness;

27—Vyadhi (व्याधि)—ailment, sickness;

28—Mati (मति)—understanding;

29—Unmada (उन्माद)—Madness;

30—Marana (मरण)—death due to extreme grief, shame or fear;

31—Vibodha (विबोध)—becoming conscious;

32—Trasa (त्रास)—fear, alarm; and

33—Vitarka (वितर्क)—reasoning, doubt.

Sentiments in Shrutis

We now come to the psychological study of music, to know its effect on the mind. For this it is necessary to investigate the inner meanings of the notes, and how by suitable combinations they can be made to express the desired feelings and generate the desired emotions. The subject was well investigated by the ancient Indian music-makers like Bharata; the impression created by each musical note was determined, and the feeling each tune gave expression to, was specified. This was later on done by personifying the tune and picturing them with particular feelings or emotions. After the time of Sharangdeva, however, the matter was, entirely neglected.

The old Indian Music makers realised this. They did not consider it enough to fix values, by some arbitrary methods, merely for the Swara notes or some of their modifications, but carefully weighed sounds at shorter intervals viz. of one shruti. For this purpose, Vinyas were constructed with twenty-two strings which were tuned to the twenty-two shrutis to facilitate comparison. The inner meaning which the sound of each shruti indicated was determined in reference to the main note, which being the natural note uttered without any exertion, represented a state of mind, peaceful and generous, and free from perturbation or extraneous influences.

The result thus obtained has been preserved in the newer names of the shrutis themselves, which new names have meanings indicated by their sounds. The following is a list of shrutis, with their meanings and derivation of the names:—

1. *Tivra* (तीव्रा) : Indicates sharpness, acuteness, violence, heat.

2. *Kumudvati* (कुमुदवती) : From Kumud—unfriendly, indicates unkindness, criticism, complaint, enmity, avarice, Kumud also means a lotus or water-lily and the shruti may express inward pleasure.

3. *Manda* (मन्दा) : From Manda—slow, apathetic, cold indicates idleness, inaction, apathy, want of pleasure or enthusiasm.

4. *Chhandovati* (छन्दोवती) : From Chhandas, free will, independent conduct indicates peace of mind, independence, heroism, generosity.

5. *Dayavati* (दयावती) : From Daya—compassion, sympathy, indicates pity, tenderness, affection.

6. *Ranjani* (रंजनी) : From Ranjan colour, pleasing, indicates pleasure, delight, appreciation.

7. *Raktika* (रक्तिका) : From Rakti—pleasingness, attachment, indicates charm, marvellousness, devotion, appreciation, state of getting impassioned.

8. *Raudri* (रौद्री) : From Raudra=heat, wrath, indicates heat, wrath, enthusiasm.

9. *Krodhi* (क्रोधी) : From Krodha=anger, indicates anger, cursing.

10. *Vajrika* (वज्रिका) : From Vajra=steel, indicates severe language, abusing, cursing.

11. *Prasarini* (प्रसारिणी) : From Prasarana—expanding, diffusing, indicates enquiry, explanation.

12. *Priti* (प्रीति) : Indicates joy, happiness, satisfaction, favour, affection.

13. *Marjani* (मार्जिनी) : Marjana=cleaning, purifying, effacing, indicates clearing one's breast, affection, joking, ridicule, egoism.

14. *Kshiti* (क्षिति) : From Kshi=to decay, to rule indicates egoism, complaint of loss.

15. *Rakta* (रक्ता) : From Rakta=to be coloured or attached, to be affected or excited, indicates attachment, devotion, excitement, worry.

16. *Sandipini* (संदीपिनी) : Sandipana=inflaming, kindling, exciting, indicates kindling of the flames of love, excitement due to same.

17. *Alapini* (अलापिनी) : From alap=to talk, indicates conversation or talk between lovers, expressions of love, affection, entreaty, sympathy.

18. *Madanti* (मदान्ति) : From Mada indicates ardent passion, affection, intoxication, madness, sexual love, arrogance, anger due to jealousy.

19. *Rohini* (रोहिणी) : From Ruh=to grow, indicates development to pleasure, pain or other feelings. The word also means a girl just grown up, and indicates hopes and fears of early life, solitary musings.

20. *Ramya* (रम्या) : From Ram=to rest, to remain quiet indicates quietness, solitude, musings, apathy, carelessness towards outward show.

21. *Ugra* (उग्रा) : From Ugra=powerful, formidable, sharp—sharpens feelings also expresses formidableness, awe, fear.

22. *Kshobhini* (क्षोभिणी) : From Kshobh=to tremble, to be agitated, disturbance, agitation, trembling, unnervedness, pitiableness, extreme worry.

Besides the above 22 shrutis two more Shrutis i.e. Sikka and Shantha have been added to new scale to make it a scale of 24 shrutis. They are taken from Naradeeya Shrutis. Sikka has been added to Re and Shantha to Dha. The sentiments of these shrutis resemble with the shrutis to which they are added.

These twenty two shrutis were divided by the old music-makers into five categories, known as:—

1. *Dipta* (दीप्ता) : expressing excitement or stimulation.
2. *Ayata* (अयाता) : showing diffusiveness, prolixity or expansion.
3. *Karuna* (करुण) : expressing compassion and pity;
4. *Mridu* (मृदु): showing tenderness of feeling;
5. *Madhya* (मध्या): being neutral and giving expression to feeling.

The shrutis coming each of these categories are as under :—

Dipta : Tivra, Raudri, Vajrika, Ugra.

Ayata : Kumudvati, Krodhi, Prasarini, Sandipini, Rohini.

Karuna : Dayavati, Alapini, Madantika.

Mridu : Manda, Rati, Preeti, Kshiti.

Madhya : Chhandovati, Ranjani, Marjini, Rakta, Ramya, Kshobhini.

With this analysis of sounds at small intervals, it would be easier to find out what sentiment each tune gives or which tune should be used to express a particular feeling.

Before coming to this, however, it is necessary to have a clear idea of the several sentiments and the feelings they produce in the mind.

Sentiments in Notes

Knowing the different sentiments and the way, they find expression as explained briefly in the previous chapter, and the expression given by each Shruti, as shown in the chapter preceding, it would be easy to assign values to each of the notes in the matter of expression, as also to their combinations in the matter different of tunes. An endeavour will be made in this and the following chapters to do this.

According to the old writers (Sharangadeva and others) Shadaja comprises the shrutis Manda, Chhandovati, Dayavati, and Ranjani. These clearly indicate Vira Rasa, so as is correctly noted as being the chief note of that sentiment. Rishabha takes Raktika and Raudri, and is not incorrectly taken as the note for Adbhuta Rasa. Gandhara comprises Krodhi. Vajrika and Prasarini preeti indicates Raudra or sentiment of anger. Madhyama and Panchama extend over Preeti, Marjini, Kshiti, Rakta, Sandipini and Alapini, and hence these two notes take up the sentiments Hasa and Shringara. Madanti, Rohini, Ramya, Ugra, Kshobhini, Tivra, and Kumudvati go to Dhaivata and Nishada which have therefore been correctly mentioned as being used in Vibhatsa, Bhayanaka and Karuna Rasas. It will thus be seen that the ancient music makers did not fix any haphazard values to the notes, but fixed them in a most scientific way.

With the old Indian music. comprising 19 notes, most of the emotions could be expressed. What could not be done was accomplished by the expert singers by lowering or raising their voices in smaller intervals than provided by the notes. In stringed instruments, like Veena and Sitar, this was done by stretching the string or wire over the frets to produce a sharper note. This is called Mid and known as quarter, half etc., according to the sharpness required, the full Mid giving the next higher note.

The present-day music having a smaller number of notes only 12 against the 19 of the old music can express the sentiments very partially and the musician must strive much harder to produce the real effect. The reduction in the number of notes has in this respect been to our great disadvantage, and has perhaps largely contributed to the disappearance of the science of expression, comprising the old Arthadhyaya from Indian music.

The twelve notes of the present-day Indian music are fixed at the shrutis noted against them and can in a composition, express the emotions indicated by the shrutis, unless the notes are sharpened or flattened.

The twelve notes of the harmonium which, as has been noticed before, have equalised intervals, represent very nearly the same shrutis as above, excepting that is nearer Krodhi than Vajrika, and nearer Kshobhini than Tivra. Here no Mid is possible and intermediate sounds are attempted by sounding two adjacent notes closely following each other with short interval repetitions. It cannot, however, produce the correct note wanted, although the effect is pleasing. This is also done in Sitar and is known as Zamzama or Gitkiri.

The following list of the nine rasas gives chief notes of the present Indian music, which are approximately appropriate for each rasa, according to the value of the shrutis given by the old writers; the Mid notes being half.

	Rasa	Note	Value of Shrutis	Shrutis
1.	Vira	Shadaja	with Mid	Manda, Chhandovati
2.	Adbhuta	Rishbha	with Mid	Dayavati & Ranjini
3.	Raudra	Gandhara	with Mid	Raktika & Roudari
4.	Hasa		with Mid	Krodhi, Vajrika & Parsarini
5.	Shringara	Madhyama	with Mid	Preeti, Marjini & Kshiti
6.	Vibhatsa	Panchama		
7.	Bhayanaka	Dhayvata		Madanti, Rohini
				Ramya, Ugra, Kshobini
8.	Karuna	Nishada	with Mid	Tivra & Kamodvati
9.	Shanta			

The notes as shown above have to be used more frequently than others, as Vadis or Samvadis, and in the form of Tanas and Alankaras, so that the particular Rasas may be expressed.

NATURAL NOTES WITH THEIR SHRUTIS

	Notes	Fixed on Shruti	Name of Shrutis
1.	Shadaja	Chhandovati	Tibra, Kumudvati, Manda, Chhandovati.
2.	Rishbha	Ratika	Sikka, Dayavati, Ranjani, Ratika.
3.	Gandhara	Karodhi	Raudri, Karodhi.
4.	Madhyama	Marjini	Vajrika, Parsarni, Preeti, Marjini.
5.	Panchama	Alapini	Kshiti, Rakta, Sandipini, Alapini.
6.	Dhaivata	Ramya	Shantha, Madanti, Rohini, Ramya.
7.	Nishada	Kshobhini	Ugra, Kshohini.

NATURAL NOTES WITH THEIR SHRUTI JATEES

Notes	Shruti	Shruti Jatees
Shadaja	Chhandovati	Deepta, Ayata, Mridu, Madhya.
Rishbha	Raktika	Karuna, Madhya, Mridu.
Gandhara	Karodhi	Deepta, Ayata.
Madhyama	Marjini	Deepta, Ayata, Mridu, Madhya.
Panchama	Alapini	Mridu, Madhya, Ayata, Karuna.
Dhaivata	Ramya	Karuna, Ayata, Madhya.
Nishada	Kshobhini	Deepta, Madhya

DESCRIPTION OF THE SHRUTI JATEES WITH NOTES

Shadja=Deepta expressing excitement or stimulation.

Ayata=Showing diffusiveness, prolixity, or expansion.

Mridu=Showing tenderness of feelings.

Madhya=Being neutral and giving expression to feelings.

Rishbha=Karuna expressing compassion and pity.

Madhya=Being neutral and giving feelings.

Mridu=Showing tenderness of feelings.

Gandhara=Deepta expressing excitement, stimulation, showing diffusiveness, prolixity expansion.

Madhyama=Deepta expressing excitement or stimulation.

Ayata=Showing diffusiveness, prolixity or expansion.

Mridu=Showing tenderness of feelings.

Madhya=Being neutral and giving expression to feelings.

Panchama=Mridu showing tenderness of feelings.

Madhya = Being neutral and giving expression to feelings.

Ayata = Showing diffusiveness, prolixity of expression.

Karuna = Expressing compassion and pity.

Dhaivata = Karuna, expressing compassion and pity.

Ayata = Showing diffusiveness, prolixity or expansion.

Madhya = Being natural and giving expression to feelings.

Nishadha = Deepta expressing excitement or stimulation.

Madhya = Being neutral and giving expression to feelings.

THE EFFECTS OF COLOURS ON NOTES

In the opinion of great Rishis the facts which are commonly beyond the clear understanding, people try to explain them with various examples and illustrations with reference to the same fact. What is the effect of musical sound on man ? How do the sentiments 'Rati' and feelings and emotions originate and how are they inter-related to each other, is clearly explained by Sri Sarang Deva in Sangeet Ratnakara. We have given a chart from Sangeet Ratnakara on page 52. The Shrutis notes and colours of notes alongwith human sound and the animal to which the sound nearly resembles.

Now the question arises whether these colours affect the human body or not. If they do so, how do they do it.

These are mainly three primary colours in nature. They are Yellow, Red and Blue. All other colours are made with the combination of these three.

According to Ayurvedic views these three colours are closely related to human body and bodily diseases such as —

(i) Yellow for Vaata (Air)
(ii) Red for Pitta (Heat)
(iii) Blue for Kabham (Phelgm)

It is the general view that the rays of the sun are of white colour but when seen through mirror they reflect seven colours—Violet, Indigo, Blue, Green, Yellow, Orange and Red.

These seven colours combine together in white. That is why the rays of the sun appear white to nacked eyes. The positive colour is white and negative is black.

Astronomy explains that every star reflects its rays on earth. The colours of the rays of these planets are as follows :—

Moon	—	Silvery white
Mars	—	Red
Mercury	—	Yellow
Jupitor	—	Orange
Venus	—	Blue
Saturn	—	Deep Blue
Naptune	—	Black
(Name of earth)		

Pluto   Sky Blue
(Shade of earth)

These seven planets at the time of revolution around the sun in orbit throw the rays of colours on earth. Owing to the different speed of revolution of various planets the effect of rays is not the same throughout the earth.

Sun is hot, Moon is cool, Mars is dry, Mercury is neutral, Jupitor is soothing. Venus is energetic and Saturn is obstructive. Hence, the intensive rays of the Sun show the effects on the same ratio.

The Nature of Seven Colours

Red   :—The nature of this colour is hot and affects the blood circulation in human body.

Yellow   :—This colour is conducive to health and energy. It refreshes memory and makes one happy.

Light Blue :—This colour is cool. It gives energy to breathing system.

Green   :—It is the combination of yellow and blue. It is useful to skin diseases.

Orange   :—It is combination of red and yellow and gives energy to respiratory system and blood circulation.

Deep Blue :—It is cool and keeps the respiration system regular. It diminishes the thirst also.

Violet   :—The nature of this colour resembles with that of deep blue. It increases the red capsules in blood.

Colours of Notes according to Sangeet-Ratnakara

1.	Sa	C	Pink	Cold and moist
2.	Re	D	Green	Cold and dry
3.	Ga	E	Orange	Cold and moist
4.	Ma	F	Purple	Hot and dry
5.	Pa	G	Red	Hot and dry
6.	Dha	A	Yellow	Hot and cold
7.	Nee	B	Black	Cold and dry

These colours are closely related to human life and the sound of notes can prove useful for eradicating the human diseases.

18

Formation of Raga

The following points should be kept in mind at the time of formation of a Raga :—

1. *Bhava*—Bhava or the sentiment is the state of mind which is excited or subsided at a particular time due to some circumstances created by some touching happening of life or incident old or new.

2. *The Prominent Character Male or Female*—The prominent incident of the Raga i.e. the season, occasion or any other essential role played in that character.

3. *Selection of Notes according to Rasas*—After selection of Rasas the musician starts tuning in himself through humming in a very light sound and establishes his Vadi and Samvadi Swaras. The Vadi Swara which is called the king note is capable to express the nature of Raga. After fixing Vadi and Samvadi Swaras (Major and Harmonic Notes) he starts to create the true picture of the Raga, Ascent, Descent and the Sanchary Varna.

4. *Song*—At the time of prolongation, some particular words of his theme automatically evolves out of his heart and make a chain of ideas and convert themselves in proper rhythm themselves.

5. *Time*—The musician sets the time of singing on the basis of nature, happening and subject matter of the songs.

To understand the theme of a Raga clearly an example is given below :—

Central Theme of the Raga

A young girl of about 17 or 18 years in the prime of her lust of life, tries to approach her lover in complete make up and full hope to win over him with all possible hopes and desires and in the agony and perplexion for the lovely embrace. She steps ahead with a steady walk. When she reaches her lover, she is not warmly welcomed by him rather scolded and treated in an insulting manner and refused the lovely meet. Being insulted and disappointed she tries to retard back with feeble and unsteady steps resulting a painful fall in isolation.

The main character of his theme is female. So the half tone notes are comparatively more effective and the harmonic notes will be fourth from the Major note. The main Rasa or the prominent sentiment is the Shrangara or the sentiment of love. The first part of which is Sambhoga which encourages the beloved towards the pleasure of holy meet and the second part which leads the beloved towards the rejection and disappointment is Vipralambha.

In Sa Re Ga Ma Pa Dha and Nee—Re, Ga, Dha and Nee are half tone notes and the remaining three are full tone notes.

Theme of Raga

Sentiments of Shrutis of Notes

1. *Shadaja* (Sa) Full tone—(Natural) Chhandovati indicates peace of mind, independence and generousity.

2. *Rishabha* (Re) Half tone—Daya Vati indicates pity, sympathy, tenderness and affection.

3. *Gandhara* (Ga) Half tone—Krodhi—indicates anger and cursing.

4. *Madhyama* (Ma) Natural—Margini indicates clearing one's breast, affection, joking, ridicule and egoism.

5. *Panchama* (Pa) Natural fixed—Alapini indicates conversation talks between lovers, expression of love and excitement.

6. *Dhaivata* (Dha) Half tone—Madanti indicates ardent passion, affection, intoxication, madness, sexual love, arrogance and anger due to jealousy.

129

7. *Nishada* (Nee) Half tone—Kshobhini—indicates disturbance, agitation, pitiableness and extreme worry.

Ascent—In ascent she is full of joy, eagerness and hope, hence tries to proceed ahead in very swift steps leaving and overlapping several nots behind such as starting from Sa touches Re Ma and Pa leaving Ga unstepped, henceforward again steps on Dha and leaving Nee takes straight way to Sa Upper Octave.

Descent—Descent is not as encouraging and hopeful as ascent was because being rejected by her lover she is feeling disappointment and disheartedness hence steps back in feeble and trembling manner. She is not so swift and hasty. So in a very slow and silent manner steps on Sa, Nee and Dha and stops at Pa and again stops at Ga giving a slight touch at Ma and then stoping at Re approaches Sa back.

If we look closely into the manner of movement in ascent and descent we will come to know that there is comparatively greater pause at Dhaivata in prolongation and being adjacent to Pancham it also expresses its sentiments. So it is supposed as a major note (Vadi Swara) and fourth note i.e. Ga behind it has been supposed as harmonic note. It makes the ascent of Audava and descent of Sampoorn Category. The remaining notes used in this Raga are categorised as Anuvadi notes such as :—

Ascent—Sa, Re, Ma, Pa, Dha, Sa

Descent—Nee, Dha, Pa, Ma, Ga. Re. Sa

The inner Bhavas (sentiments) naturally take rhythmical form and come out of his mouth as songs.

I—Karee Karun men ek pal na mane jiyara.

    Piya bin aaj ab men.

II—Din te ren bhai, ren te dina

    Rah takat hun unake awankee

    Kase kahun apane jiyara kee men.

Pakad—The Central theme of a Raga which is expected again and again to express the prominent sentiments is called the Pakad. The notes of Pakad of the Raga are given below :—

Re, Ma, Pa, Nee, Dha, Pa

The name Asavary has a clear and meaningful background behind its evolution. In olden days Asavary took its origin in Sauvery meaning thereby hundreds of enemies. After that it took the shape Asa-very having hopes and enemies to explain itself. It explains afterwards that the hopes of meeting to her lover faced hundreds of obstacles in the way of *Milan*, hence was named as Asha-very or Asha or hopes affected by enemies and became popular by enemies as Asavary before the musicians of modern times. In old time Re Komal or Half tone was used but nowa days Re of Full tone note is used.

130

19

Method of Displaying Ragas

Music is the expression of inner feelings in fine Rhythm and Laya, and how does a musician display them to audience depends upon his merits. There are some guidelines laid down by old and talented musicians for those who display their art in systematically. If a musician follows those guidelines he or she will be able to display the art more influentially.

In ancient days there were institutions of music where a student acquired knowledge and attained a certain degree of proficiency which qualified him in his profession and gave him status and position in the musical world.

An efficient singer was supposed to follow these and several other injunctions, he was also carefully instructed to impress upon the hearers with the sum climax of the song. Sum climax is the important beat or *juncture* of a tune where all the attention of the hearers is deeply concentrated. A classical song had to be presented with pleasant demeanour, and good manners, inspiring confidence as 'one who knows' to the listener, who would be impressed. The singer should also discriminate, and mark the occasion by singing opportune songs. He should have a good memory, and should be something of a poet. The musician of olden days was carefully brought up on these ideal principles. He was regulated by all the laws so appropriately and becomingly laid down for a master.

MERITS OF VOICE

The singer had to be distinguished with thirteen qualities of voice production :

1. *Mirisht* : was the voice that should affect all who hear it.

2. *Madhur* : was the very loud nor very low, but deep and rich, and that while singing he should be able to retain the breath for a long time and not suffer from short breath.

3. *Tara Sthana* : that the three saptakas should be executed with equal facility and ease.

4. *Sakhaba* : that the voice should be possessed of the power of creating laughter in the assembly.

5. *Daran* : that the voice should be possessed such pathos as to produce deep-feelings and tears.

6. *Komal* : that the voice should be soft and stirring.

7. *Sara Dak* : that the voice should be big and heard distinctly at a distance.

131

8. *Ghan* : that the voice should be clear without tremor, and possess depth.

9. *Sang Da* : was to execute all the Tanas (variations) with great ease.

10. *Gad* : that the command of voice should be so academic so as to be able to produce loud and soft sounds at will.

11. *Salohan* : was to be able to sing at length without break.

12. *Parjar* : that the singer should be of a prepossessing appearance and noble disposition, and not resort to facial and bodily contortions.

DEMERITS OF VOICE

There were several objectionable mannerisms which disqualified a singer. A long list of them is given in the sacred books. The following are a few :

1. *Sandasht* : is to sing with closed teeth.
2. *Bhut* : is to sing with fear.
3. *Sankat* : is to sing without confidence.
4. *Kampat* : is to start with a tremor in the voice.
5. *Karagi* : is to sing with mouth wide open.
6. *Kapal* : is to sing with flourished.
7. *Kagay* : is to start with commotion and noise.
8. *Karaba* : is to crane the neck like a camel.
9. *Jumbuk* : is to shake and whirl the head and neck while singing.
10. *Parsari* : is to make frantic gestures with the hands.
11. *Namiluk* : is to sing with eyes closed.
12. *Namilukm* : is to sing with eyes closed tight.
13. *Abagpat* : is to sing with all the words jumbled up together, and rolling in the throat so as to be incomprehensible.
14. *Stekarim* : is to sing by taking sharp quick breaths.
15. *San Nasik* : is that to sing with anosal tongue.
16. *Pava Chat* : is that the voice should resemble with the braying of a donkey.

The Points to Remember Before Singing a Raga

Before singing a Raga it is essential to know whether it is a male or female raga because at the time of creating rasas through Ragas the knowledge of understanding the sentiments of male or female is also essential. Males by nature possess the sentiments of heroism, self-respect and honour while females are filled with sentiments of sweetness, delicacy kindness, love and affection. Moreover they are linked more with string of love. Hence the knowledge of male or female sentiments is as essential as is the expression of song through notes.

A musician should try to draw out the clear picture of a particular Rasa in his mind. He should draw the outlines of notes of thata by singing it beforehand and should be well acquainted with full tone, half tone and sharp notes through practice. After having complete knowledge of notes one should proceed further towards its ascent and descent as it draws-the vivid picture of the outer structure of a Raga. So he should sing the notes taking every care of stoppages wherever necessary.

After understanding ascent and descent he should make the repeated practice of pakad.

To bring out clear picture of Raga prolongation is the only means for making a smooth display. The prolongation depends on the wisdom and sentiments as it has the capacity to explain the nature of Raga.

After prolongation the song of Raga should be taken in Vilambit Laya with gradual increase in Laya and Rhythm. After it the use of Tan-Paltas be made to make it more clear and understandable. This type of work in a Raga is also called the adorning of Raga.

Sangeet Ratnakara has mentioned 15 methods for pronouncing or playing notes and Shrutis. In old times it was called Gamak and was categorised in 15 groups such as 1. Tirap, 2. Sphurit, 3. Kampit, 4. Leen, 5. Andolit, 6. Valit, 7. Tribhinna, 8. Kurula, 9. Ahat, 10. Ullasit, 11. Plavit, 12. Humphit, 13. Mudrit 14. Namit and 15. Misrit.

The following types of Gamak such as Meend, Soot, Ghaseet, Kana, Pakar, Jham Jhama Gitkidi and Kampan (Andolan) are popular even today. They are expressed through vocal and instrumental musics.

Meend—The pronouncing of notes without disturbing the sound one, two, or three notes forward or backward taken from a particular note is called Meend. In old times it was called as Valit and Kurula. Valit stood for Meend and Kurula for Soot or Ghaseet. Meend in vocal music can be taken in both sides i.e. forward and backward but in instrumental music it is taken out by pulling the strings of instruments like sitar and that can be shown only of forward notes and not of backward notes. The second type of meend which is called Soot or Ghaseet can be obtained on both sides from the instruments played by bow such as Sarangee, Violen and Dilruba and also some instruments played by plastic piece like Sarod and Rubab etc. Meend is pronounced by mixing the throat and nose voices together. Meend is very essential for prolongation. The use of shrutis is very essential for meend.

Kampan—To create waves in the sound by shaking the notes is called Kampan. If the frets of the instruments are pressed lightly to produce vibrating sound it is called Kanpan. It is produced by pronouncing aa...aa...through throat in low pitch.

Andolan—Andolan is swinging of voice gracefully and appealingly loud. It is done by the movement of fingers on frets backward and forward on the stringed instruments like sitar.

Kana—Kana is the Punjabi word which means a slight pause. If at the time o₁ producing a particular note. On sitar the next note is touched slightly by the next finger and then it is turned back. The slight touch by the second finger will be called Kana. In other words we can say that Kana is the slight touch of the next note by the second finger at the time of pronouncing a particular note.

133

Pukar—The showing of sound in highpitch is called Pukar-for example if we have pronounced Sa in medium Octave and soonafter produce the same note of upper octave it will be called Pukar. It can be sung through throat and played with foot on instrument too.

Murakee—Murkee is also a Punjabi word which means the earring. If the musician shapes his sound in circular form in ascent and descent, it is called Murkee.

Raga Alapa

In old days the prolongation was done with major note as first note. It completed in 3 parts.

1. Prolongation from Major note to Harmonic note.
2. Prolongation of notes from major note to Same note of Upper Octave.
3. Prolongation from major note to same note of Upper Octave by combining them together.

Rag Alapa after wards was taken in 4 parts :—

(a) Sthai

(b) Antara

(c) Sanchary

(d) Abhog.

1. *Sthai Alapa* (I Part)—Prolongation of Sthai notes.

2. *Antara* (Second part)—Prolongation of notes from sthai to the notes of Upper Octave.

3. *Sanchary*—Prolongation of notes of Sthai and Antara together.

4. *Abhoga*—Prolongation of notes on upper octave upto high pitch.

This prolongation of four Types i.e. Sthai Antara, Sanchari and Abhog is popular now-a-days in the following manner :—

In Dhrupad Gayan Rag-Alap is played before the song but in Khayal Gayans the prolongation is done along with the song and the notes of that prolongation is as follows :—

1. Prolongation is done from Sa note to Madayam Ma. If major note is before the Madhyam Ma. Then more emphasis is given on it.

   S — RM, P — — P — — D — — P — — DM — P — MP — DMP —
   G   — — R —   S.

2. Prolongation is done in greater details from Sa to Ma of lower octave such as

   S — — R S — — N D — — N D — —

   P — — M P D P — — M — P — D — S — —

134

3. Prolongation from Sa note to Sa and Re of Upper Octave such as :—

S R M P — — D M P — — — M P — —

N D P — M P D — Ṡ — — N D — D —

P — M P D — Ṡ — Ṙ Ṡ — N D P —

M P — N — D — P — M P G — — R — S

4. If major note is before Ma than prolongation is started either from same note or from Ma or Pa to Ma or Pa of Upper Octave note such as :

M P — D — D — P — M P — N — D — D P

M P — D — Ṡ — Ṙ — S — G — R —

M Ṡ — G M — Ṙ Ṡ — — N D P M P N D P

— M P — G — R — S.

Views of Pt. Vishnu Degambar Paluskar

Raga alapa without using shrutis is considered as incomplete and uninteresting. It fails to express the nature of Raga.

Pt. Vishnu Digambar Paluskar has taken the following notes essential for Rag Alapa. (i) Shuddha (ii) Komal (iii) Atikomal (iv) Tivra (v) Tivratar (vi) Tivratam.

But in modern times people take only two i.e. Uttara and Charha. The remaining four do not show the real picture of the Raga—due to lack of under standing of difference of notes. The reason is that the nature of Raga can not be understood before the true knowledge of different notes. For example in playing Harmonium one can not produce all the notes with out having the instrument showing clear demarcation between various notes.

—(Sangeet Lekhan Paddhti)

We are also giving below the statement of the above notes for using shrutis.

The Use of Shrutis

S. No.	Shrutis	Notes	Remarks
1.	Manda	Nee Teevra	This Shruti is used through Meend to approach Sa fixed from Nee full tone.
2.	Chhandovati	Sa Fixed	
3.	Sika	Re Ati Komal	This Shruti is used as Kana at Sa and in form of Meend from Re Komal to Sa fixed.
4.	Dayavati	Re Half tone	
5.	Ranjani	Re Ati Ati Komal	This Shruti is used in form of Kana only.
6.	Rakti ka	Re Full tone	
7.	Raudri	Ga Ati Komal	This Shruti is used as Kana at Re full tone and in form of Meend from Ga Half tone to Re full tone.
8.	Krodhi	Ga Half tone	
9.	Vajrika	Ga Ati Ati Komal	This Shruti can be used in form of Kana only.
10.	Prasarini	Ga Full tone	
11.	Preeti	Ga Teevra	This Shruti can be used in form of Kana only.
12.	Marjini	Ma Full tone	
13.	Kshiti	Ma Teevra tar	This Shruti can be used in form of Kana only.
14.	Rakta	Ma Sharp	
15.	Sandeepini	Ma Teevra tam	This Shruti is used as Kanat Pa and in form of Meend to approach Ma sharp to Pa fixed.
16.	Alapini	Pa Fixed	
17.	Shantha	Dha Ati Komal	This Shruti is used in form of Kana at Pa and in form of Meend from Dha Half tone to Pa fixed.
18.	Madanti	Dha Half tone	
19.	Rohini	Dha Ati Ati Komal	This Shruti can be used in form of Kana only.
20.	Ramya	Dha Full tone	
21.	Ugra	Nee Ati Komal	This Shruti is used in form of Kana at Dha full tone and in form of Meend from Nee Half tone to Dha full tone.
22.	Kshobhini	Nee Half tone	
23.	Teevra	Nee Ati Ati Komal	This Shruti can be used in form of Kana only.
24.	Kumudavati	Nee Full tone	

Tan Palta

After prolongation a raga (melody) is sung first slowly and distinctly, then from the beat sum, (climax) a Tan, is insered in the tune and time. The process advances showing the skill of the performer by the introduction of Tanas in endless harmonious combinations, permitting full opportunity of the talent and creative power of the musician. The individual assertion thus obtained is satisfactory both to the creator and the appreciator. Tans (expansions), others than the above combinations are Alankars. Alankars are used to make this

136

Gayan more attractive and impressive. Alankar in true sence of the term is the method of making a song appealing and touching. Alankar is of two kinds :— Swar Sargam & Tan Palta.

(a) *Swara Sargam* : is used for practice such as —

Sa Re Ga Ma Pa Dha Nee Sa.

Sa Re, Sa Re, Ga. Re Ga, Re Ga, Ma.

Sa Re Ga. Re Ga Ma. or Sa Re Ga Ma etc.

It is essential to make practice of the above Sargam through throat and Instrument both.

(b) *Tan Palta* : Tan Paltas are used to make the musical display more attractive and impressive in rhythm. The popular Tanas of to day are of three types :—

Shuddha Tana—The tana, in which notes are played in regular form both in ascent and descent, is called Shudha Tana. Such as—

Sa Re Ga Ma Pa Dha Nee Sa

Sa Nee Dha Pa Ma Ga Re Sa

Koot Tana—The Tana in which the arrangement of the notes is not regular and uniform, is called Koot Tana such as :—

Sa Ga Re Re Ma Ga Dha Pa etc.

Misra Tana—The Tana which contains Shudha Tana in ascent or descent and Koot Tan in the other part, is called the Misra Tana. Such as—

Ascent — Sa Re Ga Ma Pa Dha Nee Sa

Descent — Sa Dha Ma Pa Ga Ma Re Sa etc,

Besides the above there were some tanas used in old days such as Khataka Tana, Jhataka Tana, Vakra Tana, Aachrak Tana, Sarok Tana, Ladant Tana, Spat Tana, Git Kidi Tana, Jabda Tan, Bol Tana, Alap Tana etc. Bol Tana and Alap Tana are still used in Indian Music.

Bol Tana—In Bol Tanas the words of songs are sung rhythmically.

Alap Tana—In Alap Tana songs are sung with prologation and rhythm.

The number of Koot Tanas is $1 \times 2 \times 3 \times 4 \times 5 \times 6 \times 7 = 5040$.

The method of formation of Tanas is given below.

ONE NOTE, will give you one Tan only, Sa.

TWO NOTES, will give two Tans of different varieties, A rohi (ascending from low to high). (1) sa, re, A vrohi (descending from high to low), (2) re, sa.

THREE NOTES, sa, re, ga will give you six different Tanas : (1) sa, re, ga, (2) re, sa, ga, (3) sa, ga, re, (4) re, ga, sa. (5) ga, re. sa, and (6) ga, sa, re.

The remaining tanas can be formed on the basis of above system.

20

Modern Rag System

Before the advent of That System Rag Ragini system was popular in Indian Music. The six main Ragas, 30 Raginis and their sons and son's wives were sung on the basis of Seasons. After that Pt. Vishnu Narain Bhatkhande supposing Bilawal Thata as Shuddha Thata classified the Ragas on new lines.

Rules Regarding Ragas

1. A Raga must possess at least five notes.

2. A Raga must possess its Aroha and Avaroha (ascent & descent). Such as ascent and descent of Bhairava Raga—

   S R G M, P D, N S, S N D, P M G, R S.

3. The two adjacent notes should not be omitted at a time because it increases the interval between the remaining side notes and spoils the beauty of expression.

4. Ma (F) and Pa (G) should never be omitted at a time as both of these notes are harmonic notes of Sa (c) Therefore, the presence of anyone of them is essential in a Raga i.e. if Pa is omitted Ma must remain there and if Ma is omitted Pa must be there.

5. Sa (c) note is never omitted in any Raga because it is starter note of every Raga and tune.

6. Both types of the notes i.e. full and half tone should not be used at a time in any Raga as they spoil the beauty of the Raga.

Points to remember to recognise a Raga

1. Knowledge of the notes-natural, half tone or sharp, used in that Raga.

2. Category of Raga i.e. the number of notes used in its ascent and descent. i.e. Sampooran, Shadava or Odava etc.

3. Knowledge of the Thata of a Raga.

4. The knowledge of its Vadi (King note), Samvadi (Harmonic notes), Anuvadi and Vivadi notes of a Raga.

5. The Pakad of Raga i.e. the combination of notes which represents the outline sketch of a Raga. Such as Pakad of Bhairava Raga—
S, G M, P, D, P.
—

7. The time of singing of a Raga.

Thata means scale on which several notes of the same Raga can be played. It is called after the name of the prominent Raga played there in. For example Kaliyan Thata which contains Ma sharp and all the remaining notes as full tone notes several other Ragas such as Yaman, Hamir, Kedara and Bhoopali etc. can be played on it. Kalyan Raga is the main Raga of this scale. It is also called the Thata Vachak Raga and throws its shadow on other Ragas played on this thata.

Vadi or Major note—In old days 10 types of notes were popular to understand the nature of Ragas. These 10 notes were as follows :—

1. Giraha (ग्रह)

2. Ansha (अंश)

3. Niyas (न्यास)

4. Tar (तार)

5. Mandra (मंद्र)

6. Upniyas (अपन्यास)

7. Sanyas (सन्यास)

8. Vinyas (विन्यास)

9. Bahutva (बहुत्व)

10. Alpatva (अल्पतत्व)

Out of the above 10 notes Sa note has been taken for Girah and Niyasa. Every Raga starts from Sa note and also ends on the same. The major note was named as Ansh note in old days and Jeeva and king note in medieval age. And it was supposed the Sthai note with regards to Sthai Bhava. Major note in true sence is the basic note. It expresses the theme of Raga in complete form.

Samvadi Swara or the Harmonic notes

Harmonic note is the helper note to major note. It helps the major note to express the meaning of major note. This note usually stands fifth in Ragas and fourth in Raginis from the major note.

Anuvadi or the Helper note

All the notes other than major and Harmonic notes used in Ragas are called the Anuvadi or helper notes. In medieval age these helper notes were treated as Public notes.

Vivadi or the Distorted notes

This note is prohibited note in Ragas but the expert musician some times apply this note to make their Ragas beautiful. This note remains linked with major note.

Statement of Harmonic notes

Poorvang Vadi		Uttarang Vadi	
Major	Harmonic	Major	Harmonic
Sa	Ma or Pa	Pa	Sa or R
Re	Pa or Dha	Dha	Ga or Re
Ga	Dha or Nee	Nee	Ma or Ga
Ma	Nee or Sa	Sa	Pa or Ma

Pakad of Raga—i.e. the Combination of notes which represent the out line sketch of a Raga such as Pakad of Bhairva Raga—
Sa, Ga Ma, Pa, Dha, Pa.

Knowledge of notes—Natural, Half tone or sharp used in that Raga.

Sthai Antara Sanchari and Abhog

(i) *Sthai*—Sthai means the first Part of the song. It is the opening part of the song. It starts from Shadaj upto Madhyam or Pancham.

(ii) *Antara or the second part*—It covers the middle and upper registers. It starts from Gandhar, Madhyam or Pancham upto Madhyam of Upper Octave.

(iii) *The Sanchari or the Communicating Part*—Sthai and Antara combined. It is sung by combining Sthai and Antara together.

(iv) *Abhog*—It deals with notes of higer and upper octave on high pitch.

The above four parts are sung in Dhrupad and Dhamar and in other Gayans only Sthai and Antara are used.

CATEGORIEL OF RAGAS

Deshi and Margi Music

At the time of Jati Gayan the music was divided in to two parts. The first was Deshi and the second Margi.

Deshi Music—The Deshi Ragas contained, Folk song (Lok Geets), seasonal songs and the songs which are sung at the time of ceremonial occasions i.e. marriages, festivals and birth days etc.

Margi Music—The word Margi meant the songs which lead one to salvation and hence they were mainly sung in holy temples and other places of worship. These songs included the songs of worship of God.

Both types of songs were sung on the classical grounds. In these songs one had to keep Girah, Ansh Niyas and Vinyas etc. in to consideration.

Categories of Ragas

1. *Shudh Raga* (*Natural Ragas*)—The Ragas which are complete within themselves on the basis of notes used in them, are called the Natural Ragas. They are the independent Ragas and need not assistance of any other Raga. The examples of such Ragas are Bilaval and Bhairava.

2. *Chhaya Lagat Raga* (*Reflected Ragas*)—The Ragas which are formed with the help of some other Ragas are called the Reflected Ragas such as Des Raga.

3. *Sankeerna Raga* (*Complex Raga*)—The Ragas which are formed by the union of several other Ragas are called the mixed or Sankeerna Raga such as Rag Peelu.

4. *Ashraya Raga* (*Principal Ragas*—The name of the Raga by which a Thata is called out, is pronounced as Principal Raga. The Ashraya Raga is the most prominent of all the ragas borne out of that thata and all the other Ragas are subordinate Ragas to it. The prominent Raga is cleary visible out the subordinate Ragas and Ashraya Raga is also called the Vachak Raga.

Uttam, Madhyam and Adha Ragam

Uttam Raga (Supreme Raga)—The Ragas which are not formed by the help of others are called the Uttam Ragas. These Ragas are considered to be suitable for singing and improvising such as—Raga Hindol, Raga Siri and Raga Bhairva.

Madhyam Ragas (Ragas of Medium Category)—these are the Ragas which do not contain the clear improvisation magnitude in themselves.

Adham Ragas (Ragas of Low Categories)—These Ragas as the name denotes are the Ragas of lower category. They are formed mixed with other Ragas and are not clear in demarkating their own note hence are difficult to be managed such as Shankara, Deva Gandhary and Narainy etc.

The categories of Ragas are divided on number of notes i.e.—Sampoorna, Shadava & Odava etc. categories are given below :—

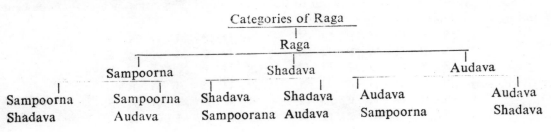

141

1. *Sampoorna Category*:—The Raga which contains seven notes in ascent and descent is called the Raga of Sampoorna category.

2. *Shadava Category*:—The Raga which contains six notes in ascent and descent is called the Raga of Shadava category.

3. *Audava Category*:—The Raga which contains five notes in ascent and descent is called the Raga of Audava category.

Besides the above three main categories, there are six more categories of Ragas. They are formed by the combination of any two of the above in ascent and descent are called by the name of which they have been combined together such as:—

4. *Sampoorana-Shadava*:—Having seven notes in ascent and six notes in descent.

5. *Sampoorana Audava*:—Having seven notes in ascent and five notes in descent.

6. *Shadava Sampoorna*:—Having six notes in ascent and seven notes in descent.

7. *Shadava Audava* :—Having six notes in ascent and five notes in descent.

8. *Audava Sampoorna* :—Having five notes in ascent and seven notes in descent.

9. *Audava Shadava* :—Having five notes in ascent and six notes in descent.

It should be remembered well that ascent will be spoken first, and the descent afterwards for example if five notes are used in ascent and seven in descent, it will be categorised as Audava Sampoorna. Besides the above nine categories of Ragas there are three more categories such as :

(a) *Sampoorna-Sampoorna*—Having seven notes in ascent and seven notes in descent

(b) *Shadava-Shadava* —Having six notes in ascent and six notes in descent.

(c) *Audava-Audava* —Having five notes in ascent and five notes in descent.

As is apparent from the name the number of notes in ascent and descent is the same but the difference is only of change of type of the notsi.e. if in ascent and descent the numbers of notes are seven each with the difference of *Nee* of half tone in place of *Nee* of full tone note in ascent or descent. It will be called the Raga of Sampoorna-Sampoorna category. The same is true with regards to Shadava-Shadava & Audava-Audava. Thus thousands of Ragas are formed with the combination of full tone and half tone notes, but we are giving only the number of Ragas having full tone notes.

Sampoorna Category

There is only one Raga of Sampoorna—Sampoorna category such as :
S R G M P D N — N D P M G R S.

Shadava category

Six Ragas of Shadava category out of full tone notes. The notes in ascent & descent are uniformly the some such as :—

1. S X G M P D N — N D P M G X S
2. S R X M P D N — N D P M X R S
3. S R G X P D N — N D P X G R S
4. S R G M X D N — N D X M G R S
5. S R G M P X N — N X P M G R S
6. S R G M P D X — X D P M G R S

Ragas of Audava Category

Fifteen Ragas of Audava category are formed out of natural notes. The notes used are uniformly the same in ascent and descent :—

```
 1.  S  X  G  M  P  D  X  —  X  D  P  M  G  X  S
 2.  S  X  G  M  P  T  N  —  N  T  P  M  G  X  S
 3.  S  X  G  M  X  D  N  —  N  D  X  M  G  X  S
 4.  S  X  G  X  P  D  N  —  N  D  P  X  G  X  S
 5.  S  X  X  M  P  D  N  —  N  D  P  M  X  X  S
 6.  S  R  X  M  P  D  X  —  X  D  P  M  X  R  S
 7.  S  R  X  M  P  X  N  —  N  X  P  M  X  R  S
 8.  S  R  X  M  X  D  N  —  N  D  X  M  X  R  S
 9.  S  R  X  X  P  D  N  —  N  D  P  X  X  R  S
10.  S  R  G  X  P  D  X  —  X  D  P  X  G  R  S
11.  S  R  G  X  P  X  N  —  N  X  P  X  G  R  S
12.  S  R  G  X  X  D  N  —  N  D  X  X  G  R  S
13.  S  R  G  M  X  D  X  —  X  D  X  M  G  R  S
14.  S  R  G  M  X  X  N  —  N  X  X  M  G  R  S
15.  S  R  G  M  P  X  X  —  X  X  P  M  G  R  S
```

If the categories of ascent and descent are changed the number will be as follows :—

1.	Sampoorna-Sampoorna	1×1 =	1
2.	Sampoorna-Shadava	1×6 =	6
3.	Shadava-Sampoorna	6×1 =	6
4.	Sampoorna-Audava	1×15 —	15
5.	Audava-Sampoorna	15×1 —	15
6.	Shadava-Shadava	6×6 —	36
7.	Shadava-Audava	6×15 —	90
8.	Audava-Shadava	15×6 —	90
9.	Audava-Audava	15×15 —	225
		Total =	484

There are 484 Ragas of natural notes. If we form Ragas by the combination of half tone and sharp notes the number will be in thousands.

Time Theory

The time theory in Indian music is the most essential part of Indian music, as it is closely related to it from the very old times. In old days the time for Raga Gayan was determined on the basis of seasons. The popular Ragas of that time were six and every Raga was sung for about two months. The 24 hours duration of the complete day was divided into 8 parts of 3 hours each.

The time theory of modern music is given as below :—
1. **Ragas of day and night**
    (a) Poorvang or Purva Ragas—(From 12 noon to 12 mid night).
    (b) Uttarang or Uttar Ragas —(From 12 mid night to 12 noon).
2. **Ragas aceording to Vadi Note (Major or King note)**
    Poorvang Vadi Note—The Ragas which have their Vadi Swara (major note in first half of the octave i.e. in Sa Re Ga Ma are called the Poorvang Vadi Ragas.

Uttarang Vadi Notes—The Ragas which have their vadi swara (Major note) in the second half of the octave i.e. in Pa, Dha, Nee and Sa are called the Uttarang Vadi Notes.

Note— Some Ragas are of different nature. In spite of having their vadi swara in uttarang they are sung in Poorvang. For such Ragas the scope of vadi note is extended upto Pa in Poorvang and upto Ma in Uttarang. i.e. Sa Re Ga Ma and Pa in Poorvang and Ma Pa Dha Nee Sa in uttarang.

3. **Time Theory According to Notes**
The duration of day and night is divided into 3 parts
    (i) 12 to 4—Ragas of day time.
    (ii) 4 to 7—Sandhi Prakash Raga i.e. Ragas of Twilight and Down. (Meeting of day and night).
    (iii) 7 to 12—Ragas of Night Time.
The details of notes and their Ragas are given below :—

Time of Singing of Ragas

S. No.	Time	Notes used in Ragas	Ragas of the Thatas to be Sung
1.	12 Noon to 4 P.M.	Re and Dha full tone (Re and Ga full tone, Nee full tone or half tone).	Kaffee, Asavari, Bhairavi and Todi
2.	4 P.M. to 7 P.M.	Re & Dha half tone (Re half tone, Ga & Nee full tone)	Puravi, Marva, Bhairava
3.	7 P.M. to 12 mid-night	Ga & Nee half tone (Ga half tone, Re and Dha half tone or full tone)	Kalyan, Bilaval and Khamaj
4.	12 mid-night to 4 A.M.	Re and Dha full tone (Re and Ga full tone, Nee full tone or half tone).	Kaffee, Asavari, Bhairavi, Todi
5.	4 A.M. to 7 A.M.	Re and Dha half tone (Re half tone, Ga & Nee full tone).	Purvi, Marva, Bhairavi
6.	7 A.M. 12 Noon	Ga & Nee half tone (Ga half tone, Re and Dha full tone or Half tone).	Kalyan, Bilaval and Khamaj

*Note :—*At the time of singing the consideration of seasons is very essential.

21

Types of Songs

Dhrupad : Dhrupad is the best type of Gayaki (song in classical music). In 13th century A.D. in time of Sarangdeva the Jati Gayan was more popular and after Jati Gayan the Dhrupad style of singing came into practice.

This type of composition and style of singing has its origin from Raja Man Singh cf Gwalior. He is considered as the founder of Dhrupad style of singing and most proficient composer as well as great pattern of it. It is sung in slow rhythm.

It contains four parts—Sthai (First part), Antara (Second part), Sanchari (Third part) and Abhoga (Fourth part). The language of Dhrupad is high and thoughts are deep. The Tan—Paltas are not used in it. This Gayan needs a forceful voice and throat, hence it is mainly sung by the male musicians.

Veer, Shanti and Shrangar Rasas are prominent in this type of songs. The central theme of this Gayan contains the ideas of self-reliance and songs of devotion to God and is mainly sung in Chautala and oblique Talas.

Dhamar : The songs sung in Dhamar tala are called Dhamar. It is a kind of Hori. A Dhamar depicts the picture of life activities of Sri Krishna just like Ras Leelas which are sung to display the life activities of Radha and Krishna in month of Falgun of Vikram era. Shrangar Rasa is more prominent in this Raga and contains four parts Sthai, Antra, Sanchari and Abhog like Dhrupad Gayan. These gayans are sung in Gamak, Meend, Boltalas and in Duggan, Chuggan. It also requires a forceful sound.

Khayal: Khayal is the word derived from Urdu language which carries thoughts as its meanings. This Gayan is very popular now-a-days. If thought deeply the Khayal Gayan is the mixture of Nibaddha and Anibaddha Gayan of old days. The Anibaddha Gayan was sung in form of prolongation without time and rhythm. Khayal Gayan came in practice by combining the Anibaddha Gayan with Nibaddha Gayan. Amir Khusro tried to popularise this Gayan, but it could not complete with Dhrupad Gayan, which continued for long time. After this in period of Mohammed Shah Adarang and Sadarang took interest in popularising the Khayal Gayan. Khayal Gayan is of two types :—

(a) Bada Khayal (Slow Khayal).

(b) Chhota Khayal (Fast Khayal).

145

Bada Khayal is sung in Vilambit Laya, Teentala, Ektala and Aada Chautal, while Chhota Khayal in Teentala, Jhaptala and Ektala. Shrangar rasa plays the prominent role in this Gayan. How does the musician express his art by prologation in this Gayan depends mostly on the individual efforts of the musician himself. The poetic words are not given importance in comparison with prolongation.

Thumari: The Thumari Gayan was started from the Nawab families near about 200 years ago. It is sweet and popular like Khayal Gayaki but the musician is not expected to maintain correctness and purity of Raga like Khayal Gayaki. Beauty expresses the prominent part. Thumari is sung in Kafee, Bhairavi and Khamaj etc. Ragas in Teen Tal, Kaharva and Dadara etc. Thumaries mainly depict the life activities of Radha and Krishna. The Thumary Gayans are more popular in Brij mandal and in eastern U.P.

The Thumari Gayans are divided into two parts *i.e.* First Part (Sthai) and second part (Antra). The use of Tan Paltas makes the Gayan more beautiful.

Tappa: Tappa Gayan was originated by Miyan Shori in 16th century A.D. The manner of singing this song resembles with that of Thumari and is divided in two parts—the Sthai and Antra (first and the second). The language of Tappa is mostly Punjabi, hence, is more popular in Punjab State. The Shrangar Rasa plays the prominent role in this Gayan. Tan Paltas are also commonly used.

Lakshan Geet : The gayan which tells us the Lakshana or the special features of a Raga, is called the Lakshana Geet *i.e.* the Lakshana Geet makes us known with the name and category of Raga its ascent and descent notes (Vadi-Samvadi notes) and the time of singing etc. The Lakshana Geet is sung in time and rhythm of the Raga to which it belongs. The Lakshana Geet clearly explains the special features of its mother Raga.

(1) *Sargam* : Sargam Gayan is the rhythmical representation of notes in the shape of songs and the Ragas which are properly controlled by proper time and rhythm, are called the Sargam Gayan.

(2) *Tarana* : This Gayan is sung through the words like Tom, Tana, Ta, Der, Da and Nee instead of songs, is called Tarana. This Gayan is rhythmical and correctness of Raga is the chief characteristic of this Gayan. The musicians now-a-days sing this song for recreation only. Tarana was started in times of Allauddin Khilji who originated it to impart the musical education to the foreigners who were not familiar with Indian language and the musical symbols etc. Hence he taught them Ragas through the above bols.

Trivat : The Gayan which contains Shabad (poetical words) Sargam and bols of Tabla and is sung in proper rhythm in Raga, is called the Trivat.

Chatrang : The Gayan which contains Shabad (poetic words) Sargam, Tarana and Bols of Tabla and is sung in Raga and in proper rhythm is called the Chatrang Gayan.

Raga Mala : In olden days the musicians used to sing through Raga Malas for making their Ragas attractive and appealing. The Ragas are sung separately in Raga Mala Gayans and every line in the song has its own Tala and Raga but the last line is linked with the Raga and Tala of the first line. This type of Raga is also called the Raga Guldasta.

Ghazal : Ghazal Gayan was started in time of Mughal Emperors. It contains two parts Sthai (First part) and Antra (Second part). The language of Ghazal is Urdu. It is sung in three ways :—

(1) Ghazal of Tala in Sthai only.
(2) Ghazal with Tala like Khayal gayan.
(3) Kavvali.

Ghazal of Half Part Tala—The second part of Ghazal is without Tala and the first part is started in drut laya (fast rhythm). The singing of Ghazal in Drut laya after the second part appears attractive.

Ghazal in Complete Talas—It is often sung in Dadara of Kaharva. The time of rhythm in the first and second part is the same. The beauty of the Ghazal is made attractive by various types of Bols of Ghazal.

Kavvali : In Kavvali Gayan too, the first part of the song or Ghazal is sung in Drut laya as in the Ghazal of half Tala. But the difference is that the former is sung by one musician while the latter by a group of musicians. The Kavvali is accompanied by the Talis (clapping).

Bhajan : The Bhajan Gayan was started in the Bhakti Kal of Medieval period. Soor, Tulsi, Kabir and Mira are the main characters of Bhakti Kal.

The Bhakti Gayans or the Bhajans contain the ideas of devotion to achieve salvation and also of courage and sacrifice. The Bhajan Gayans are of four types :—

(a) Bhajans

(b) Keertan

(c) Sankeertan

(d) Nagar Keertan.

These Bhajan Gayans are sung in Dadara, Kaharva and Teen Talas.

Bhajan : is sung by one man only.

Keertan : Keertan Gayan is sung by one or two musicians at a time.

Sankeertan : Sankeertan is the Bhakti Gayan sung by a group of musicians sitting together at a particular place.

Nagar Keertan : Nagar Keertan is the Bhakti Gayan sung by a group of musicians by wandering in streets and lanes for religious preaching.

Sabad : Sabad in ordinary language is a combination of letters having some meaning but a Sabad in music means the Vaani or the teachings of Guru Granth Sahib i.e. when the Vaani of Guru Granth Sahib is sung in musical rhythm it is called Sabad. The musical songs besides the Vanies of Guru Granth Sahib, sung in Gurdwaras are called the musical poem. The Guru Granth Sahib contains the description of all the Ragas and every Sabad contained in Guru Granth Sahib is based on any sort of Raga.

Naat : This Gayan was started by Soofi Sampradaya. Naat is a type of music in which Muslim devotees express the life activities of their Pagambar, Nabi and Rasool or they pay homage to them. It is a sort of Bhajan and its music is in form of Gazal or Kavvali type.

Geet : Means a poem having musical rhythm hence every type of poem containing a musical rhythm is known as a Geet but there are some songs which are given a particular name of Geet such as dholak Geet and marriage geet etc. Besides the modern film song are also called Geets. In Geet Gayans a musician tries to attract the audience through his musical expressions without caring for the rules and regulations of a Raga. The language of Geet is Hindustani.

22

Indian Musical Instruments and Talas

SANGEET (vocal, instrumental music and dancing), came into being with the creation of humanity as an essential part of their existence. In India from ancient times music had attained a high form of perfection, mystic, philosophic and scientific. The inventions and practices attributed to the Divinities.

Four types of instruments are used in Indian music :
1. Tata Jati (String Instruments).
2. Vitata Jati (String Instrument)
3. Sushir Jati (Wind Instruments)
4. Ghana Jati (Percussion Instruments).

Tata Jati comprises of those instruments which have long necks, set with brass or steel frets, and have groups of wires of steel, brass, cord and guts, to be struck by finger nails, Mizrab, pieces of ivory, wood, brass or steel and the long neck set on gourds, sometimes with brass plates, as the case may be. The instruments belonging to this group are : Rudra Veena, Saraswati Veena, Sur Veena, Sur Bahar, Sur Singar, Rubab, Sarod, Sitar, Tambura and Ektara.

Vitata Jati : comprises of those instruments, which have long necks, set with frets sometimes, and skins stretched on the hollow squarish frames, having groups of wires of brass, st el or gut, as the case may be, to be played with a bow. The instruments belonging to this group are : Sarangi, Kamancha, Sazinda, Taus, Dilruba, Israj and Dotara.

Sushir Jati : comprises of the pipe of Bamboos or wood like instruments to be blown by the mouth by half, or full breaths viz : Sehnai, Tootee, Nay, Bansri, Nafri, Algoza, Pungi, Singha and Shankha.

Ghana Jati : comprises of the drum like species, struck by the hands, elbows, iron rods, or wooden sticks, viz., Pakhavaj, Tabla, Nakkara, Dhol, Duff, Khanjari and Damru.

The details of Talas played on percussion instruments are given ahead :—

Tala & Laya (Time & Rhythm)

The secret of the gravitation of the Universe, the poise, balance and discipline of the movement of the heavans and earth is symbolically and mystically the result of Rhythmic Motions. Rhythm is the essence of music. The production of tones, at regular beats, is the law and order of music. In Indian music there are two kinds of rhythms. (One is Tala and the other is Laya).

Tala (Time), is an important factor regulating the relative durations of musical sounds, a mathematical proportion of equal returning values of symmetrical beats. Tal, comprises of vibrations, and vibrations are based upon the beat of human pulse, hence Tal passes with human life itself. Tal is an abbreviated form of Tandava, and Lasya, Ta, for Tandava and La for Lasya, Mahadeva and Parbati danced in ecstacy to the rhythm of the Universe, Mahadeva's dance was called Tandava, and Parbati's response was called Lasya. The combined musical measure was called Tala, which was played on Pakhavaj, Mirdang, Dhol, Nakkara, Duff, Khanjari and Tabla etc. are the instruments used for the purpose of Tala. Out of these musical instruments tabla is most popular.

The late Indian musicians invented many talas of different matras (Strokes), Khand (Bars) and Boles (words) and fixed the points of 'Sam' Talis and Khalis for every Tala.

Matra (Stroke)—A matra is taken as the shortest time in which a syllable can be properly pronounced, in medium Rhythm the time of a matra is presumed to be one second, in fast Rhythm half second and in slow Rhythm two seconds.

Boles—Sound produced by Tabla Dhama or Duggi by the stroke of fingers and hand in different ways is called boles i.e. Ta, Na Tee, Tin, Ke, Ge, Te, Tay, Dha, Dhe, Dhin.

Theka—The round of a Tala has fixed matras and on every matra there are fixed boles. They are called Thekas.

Tali—Clapping of hands is called Tali i.e. Theka of Talas having Tali points marked 1 2 3 4 etc.

Khali—Khali means a gap of some matras which boles of Theka play right hand on Tabla only. The left (Duggi or Dhama) remains silent in Khali matra's time.

Khali points help the classical musicians to understand the starting point of their Tala (Sam point) when they sing Khayal. For Khali point on Theka 'O' sign on the matra point is shown in every Tala.

Sam—The starting point of Talas called sam. Say first matra of talas is sam point and on every theka it is shown by+sign.

Laya (Rhythm or Speed)

Laya (Rhythm) in ordinary sense laya means Rhythm or speed or any regular movement to complete a circle in a definite time, it is natural harmonious flow of vocal and instrumental sound and also a regular succession of accent. According to the observations three types of Rhythm have been accepted in Indian music. All the percussion instruments are used to control and regularise the musical sound. The three types of Rhythm are :

A—*Madhya Laya* (Medium or Normal Rhythm)

B—*Drut Laya* (Quick or Fast Rhythm).

C—*Vilambit Laya* (Slow Rhythm).

150

Normal Rhythm—Normal Rhythm is the time required by musician to complete a Round or a circle of a part of song, tune or dance in easy way without any exertion. Normal rhythm is the base of the remaining two Rhythms i.e. fast and slow Rhythm.

Fast Rhythm—Fast Rhythm means half the time of normal Rhythm i.e. if a musician requires one minute time to complete a part of song, tune or dance, in normal Rhythm, he will require half of the time taken by the normal Rhythm, in other words we can say that the musician can take two rounds of his definite part of play in the time required in the normal Rhythm.

Slow Rhythm—In slow Rhythm a musician takes double the time to complete the round required by the medium or normal Rhythm. Suppose, if he completes a round of his play in one minute in normal Rhythm he will take two minutes to complete the same round.

The rhythm and the movements in Indian music have been given in a particular way i.e. some of the movements have been taken from the animals, some from birds, while some have been taken from the festivals. Such as :

(a) Teen Tal   from Horse.
(b) Chartal or Ek Tal   —   From the movement of Elephant.
(c) Sath Ke Bols of Char Tala   —   From the movement of Deer.
(d) Deep Chandi and Chanchal   —   From Hori festival.
(e) Dhamar & Aada Chautal   —   From Hori occasion in a Royal family.
(f) Jhapa Tala   —   From the movement of Camel.
(g) Sool   —   From the movement of Sparrow.
(h) Dadra   —   From the movement of Pigeon.

Talas of 16 Matras

Before singing a particular song one should take a great care of its movements.

Teen Tala

Teen Tala & Talwara contain 16 Matras and 4 Bars of 4 Matras each. They have 3 Talis and one Khali. Teen Tala is played with Chhota Khayals and Bhajans etc. while Talwara and Punjabi Theka with Bara Khayals.

Talas of 14 Matras

1. Deep Chandi
2. Jhumra
3. Dhamar
4. Aada Chautal

The Tali, Khali and Bols of each talas differ with one another. Out of them Deep Chandi Jhumara or Chanchal are played with Hori songs and local festivals. Dhamar and Aada Chautal are sung in Hori season in Royal Courts.

Talas of 12 Matras

These are two Talas of 12 Matras.

(a) Ek Tala

(b) Char Tala.

The Matras, Bars and Tali—Khali are equal.

Ek-tala is played with Bada Khayals while Chartal with Dhrupad Gayans.

Talas of 10 Matras

They are of 2 types :

(1) Jhap Tala

(2) Sool Fakhta

The Matras of both Talas are equal but the Bars, Tali and Khali are different. Besides this Keharva of 8 and 4 Matras, Dadara of 6 Matras, Tivra and Roopak of 7 Matras are played with Bhajans, Geets and Ghazals etc.

BOLES OF THEKA TAL TEEN

+				2				0				3			
1	2	3	4	5	6	7	8	9	10	11	12	13	14	15	16
Dha	Dhin	Dhin	Dha	Dha	Dhin	Dhin	Dha	Dha	Tin	Tin	Ta	Ta	Dhin	Dhin	Dha

BOLES OF THEKA TALA TEEN (Type 2)

Sam +				Tali 2				Khali 0				Tali 3			
1	2	3	4	5	6	7	8	9	10	11	12	13	14	15	16
Na	Dhi	Dhi	Na	Na	Dhi	Dhi	Na	Na	Tee	Tee	Na	Na	Dhi	Dhi	Na

BOLES OF THEKA TALWARA

Sam +				Tali 2				Khali 0				Tali 3			
1	2	3	4	5	6	7	8	9	10	11	12	13	14	15	16
Dha	Tarik	Dhin	Dhin	Dha	Dha	Tin	Tin	Ta	Trik	Dhin	Dhin	Dha	Dha	Dhin	Dhin

BOLES OF THEKA TAL DEEPCHANDI

Sam +			Tali 2				Khali 0			Tali 3			
1	2	3	4	5	6	7	8	9	10	11	12	13	14
Dha	Dhin	—	Dha	Ge	Tin	—	Ta	Tin	—	Dha	Ge	Dhin	—

BOLES OF THEKA TAL JHUMRA

Sam +			Tali 2				Khali 0			Tali 3			
1	2	3	4	5	6	7	8	9	10	11	12	13	14
Dhin	Dhin	Nak	Dhin	Dhin	Dhage	Tirkit	Tin	Tin	Nak	Dhin	Dhin	Dhage	Tirkit

BOLES OF THEKA TAL ARACHAWTAL

Sam +		Tali 2		Khali 0		Tali 3		Khali 0		Tali 4		Khali 0	
1	2	3	4	5	6	7	8	9	10	11	12	13	14
Dhin	Trik	Dhin	Na	Too	Na	Ka	Ta	Trik	Dhin	Na	Dhin	Dhin	Na

BOLES OF THEKA TAL DHAMAR

Sam					Tali		Khali			Tali			
+					2		0		3	3			
1	2	3	4	5	6	7	8	9	10	11	12	13	14
Ka	Dhi	Ta	Dhi	Ta	Dha	—	Ga	Dhee	Na	Dee	Na	Ta	—

BOLES OF THEKA TAL CHAR TAL

+		0		2		0		3			4	
1	2	3	4	5	6	7	8	9	10	11		12
Dha	Dha	Din	Ta	Kit	Dha	Din	Ta	Tit	Kat	Gadi		Gina

BOLES OF THEKA TAL EK TAL

+		0		2		0		3			4	
1	2	3	4	5	6	7	8	9	10	11		12
Dhin	Dhin	Dhage	Tirkit	Too	Na	Ka	Ta	Dhage	Tirkit	Dhin		Na

BOLES OF THEKA TAL JHAPA

+		2			0		3		
1	2	3	4	5	6	7	8	9	10
Dhin	Na	Dhin	Dhin	Na	Tin	Na	Dhin	Dhin	Na

BOLE OF THEKA TAL SOOL

+		0		2		3		0	
1	2	3	4	5	6	7	8	9	10
Dha	Dha	Din	Ta	Kit	Dha	Tit	Kit	Gadi	Gina

BOLES OF THEKA TAL DHUMALI

+				0			
1	2	3	4	5	6	7	8
Dha	Dhin	Na	Tin	Trak	Dhin	Dhage	Trak

BOLES OF THEKA TAL KAWALI

+				0			
1	2	3	4	5	6	7	8
Dhin	Dhin	Dha	Dha	Tin	Tin	Tha	Tha

BOLE OF THEKA TAL KEHARWA

+				0			
1	2	3	4	5	6	7	8
Dha	Ge	Na	Tee	Ta	Ke	Dhin	Na

BOLES OF THEKA TAL KEHARWA (Type 2)

+		0	
1	2	3	4
Dhage	Nage	Take	Dhin

BOLES OF THEKA TAL TIVRA

+			2		3	
1	2	3	4	5	6	7
Dha	Tirak	Dhi	Na	Tirak	Dhi	Na

BOLES OF THEKA TAL ROOPAK

+			2		3	
1	2	3	4	5	6	7
Tin	Tin	Na	Dhin	Na	Dhin	Na

BOLES OF THEKA TAL PASHTO

+			2		0	
1	2	3	4	5	6	7
Tin	—	Nak	Dhin	—	Dha	Ga

BOLES OF THEKA TAL DADRA

+			0		
1	2	3	4	5	6
Dha	Dhin	Na	Dha	Tin	Na

BOLES OF THEKA TAL DADRA (TYPE 2)

×			0		
1	2	3	4	5	6
Dha	Dhin	Dha	Dha	Tin	Ta

23

Music Notation-System

The system by which we get the knowledge of Notes, Octaves, Meend, Gamak Tune and Rhythm etc. is called the notation system or swara lipi. We shall not be wrong if this notation system is supposed to be the language of music. As we become familiar with one another by the medium of language of music, in the same way we get the knowledge of ascent, descent, stopage, and movement of notes by the notation system. We can play and sing very easily the songs of musicians of past with this notation system used by them even today in the same tune and rhythm. This language of music or notation system is a bit more difficult than the common language, as the former gives the knowledge of every form of sound i.e. Shruti, Note, Tune, Rhythm, Gamak and Meend etc. while the latter is only the medium of passing over the ideas of one man to another.

The Notation System which is commonly used in Indian Music now-a-days is not much old. The musicians of olden time did not pay much attention towards the Notation System. Had they adopted some proper Notation System, we would have not missed the valuable Gayakis of Gopal Nayaka, Swami Haridas, Tansen, Baiju Bavara and Adaranga-Sadaranga to-day.

The Oral System of musical education was also used in the past. The student has to learn the Ragas and Raginis by heart, sitting years together in shelter of their Gurus. The writing system was not much popular in those days and the experts of various subjects did not believe in written system of instructions. That is why oral system of learning by heart did not pass over its originality to the next generations. So little by little it faced many changes and many of the Ragas disappeared at all.

Since 11th Century A.D. the foreign invasions started over India. That continued up to 19th century and people had to lead an unrestful life. These unavoidable historical circumstances diverted the attention of musicians from musical taste and no appreciable efforts were made to improve the notation system. After the end of Muslim rule over India, Sharmae Ishrat was published in 1874 in Urdu language. The book adopted the notation system on the basis of number of frets for playing Sitar. The Talies are shown by a special sign. The other Urdu publications of that time using same type of notation system are Nagmae-Sitar, Tahsilul Sitar and Nad Vinod Grantha followed by Sangeet Sar. In these books the notes were divided in three groups on the basis of Octaves.

In 1901 Pt. Vishnu Digambar Paluskar established Gandharva Mahavidyalaya in Lahore (now in Pakistan) and started to impart musical education through new system of music notations. The notes of this system Here also divided into Three groups on the basis of

155

Octaves and various types of signs were used to show full tone, half tone and sharp notes. But afterwards to solve the problem of difficulty due to varieties of sign notes for the learners the Gandharva Mahavidalaya adopted the reformed and modified notation system. It will not be exaggeration if we call Pt. Vishnu Digambar Paluskar as the originator of Indian music notation system because after Sangeet Ratnakara no notation system could suit itself to impart proper education to children. Pt. Vishnu Digambar Paluskar was the first man to use the notation system in Indian musical education*.

After this Pt. Vishnu Narain Bhatkhande used new type of notation system and collected songs of all the musicians and gave them proper order. The basic principles of this notation system are as follows:—

NOTATION SYSTEM

(Pt. Vishnu Digambar Paluskar).

Full Tone Note—No Sign. S R G M P D N
Half Tone & Sharp Note-Oblique line under the notes

$$\underset{|}{R} \quad \underset{|}{G} \quad \underset{|}{M} \quad \underset{|}{D} \quad \underset{|}{N}$$

Medium Octave—No Sign.   S R G M P D N

Lower Octave—A dot on the notes.

$$\dot{N} \quad \dot{D} \quad \dot{P} \quad \dot{M}$$

Upper Octave notes—A vertical line on the notes.

$$\overset{|}{S} \quad \overset{|}{R} \quad \overset{|}{G} \quad \overset{|}{M}$$

Sam 1—Under the note

Tali 2 3 4 under the note.

Khali+under the note.

Division of Matras—Different signs are used.

NOTATION SYSTEM

(Pt. Vishnu Narain Bhatkhande)

Pt. Vishnu Narain Bhatkhande has given a very clear and easy notation system. He invented a new notation system and brought a drastic change in Indian Music. In his book 'Hindustani Sangeet Kramik Pustak', written in 6 Volumes, is a sound proof of the fact that he has done a marvellous work in musical world. In Indian University education his notation system has been made a base for the musicial instruction in higher education of the subject.

---

* For details of Notation systems read the History of Indian Music notation system by the same author.

Full Tone Note—No sign.   S R G M P D N

Half Tone Note—A horizontal line under the notes. R G D N
                                                   — — — —

Sharp Note—A vertical line on the note   M

Medium Octave—No sign. S R G M P D N

Lower Octave—A Dot under the note. N D P M
                                    . . . .

Upper Octave—A Dot over the note Ṡ Ṙ Ġ Ṁ

Sam   +
Tali   1—2—3—4
Khali   0

The Foreign Notation System

After the spread of British rule over India the staff notations were used in military bands, and the practice in English medium schools was done on these lines. This type of practice is still going on. After independence this staff notation moved towards the film and very soon it got such a high popularity that it became the super most liking of the young generation. It is, therefore, essential to mention this system, along with the Indian Notation System.

The foreign notation system changed with the change of time and with the difficulties faced by the musicians time after time. In this historical evolution of staff notation system the following system came in practice time after time.

1. SELF NOTATION—In this notation system the westerners used Do, Re, Me, Fa, La and Si place of Sa Re Ga Ma Pa Dha Nee.

2. NEUMES NOTATION—In this system the signs of stop, half stop, desh and other lines of various types were used.

3. CHEVE NOTATION—In this system the figures like 1 2 3 and 4 etc. are taken as a help to express notes.

4. STAFF NOTATION—It is the modified way of Neumes System and has been made easier to make it understandable by the common people.

The signs of Foreign Notation System explain three essential factors :—

A. Time.

B. Notes.

C. Octave.

Time Signs :—

When these time signs are put over the lines, become notes. To show these two clefs of 5 long lines have been supposed. The first is the Treble Clef and the Second is the Bass Clef. In between these two clefs is a centre line which divides both the clefs. The medium and the upper octave notes are shown on Treble Clef and lower and double lower octaves on

157

Bass Clef. When we put some sign over the clef below the centre line, which is called the Bass Clef, they become the notes of lower and double lower octaves. The position of Signs on these clefs is as follows :—

When Signs are put to express notes, some of them cut the line and some of them remain between the lines. The position can be understood as given in Sketch.

TALAS IN ENGLISH MUSIC

Bars are used in English Notation system. The number of time notes in a particular bar depends upon the number of strokes. We put as many time notes in a particular bar as is the number of strokes in it.

According to the time they may be of two, three or four strokes. The time signs are written along with the clef sings. In staff notation a four strokes bar has been made as the base and the time signature is written as :—

1. 1 Beat time
2. 1/2 Beat time
3. 1/4 Beat time
4. 1/8 Beat time
5. 1/16 Beat time
6. 1/32 Beat time
7. Full Tone Notes
8. Half Tone Notes
9. Shap Note

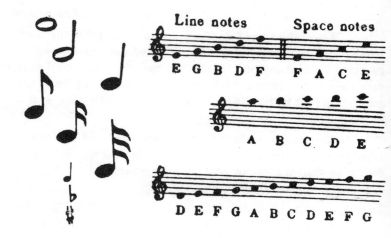

Line notes   Space notes

E G B D F   F A C E

A B C D E

D E F G A B C D E F G

$\dfrac{2}{4}, \dfrac{3}{4}$ and $\dfrac{4}{4}$. It explains as follows :—

$\dfrac{2}{4}$ means 2 Strokes in every bar.

$\dfrac{3}{4}$ means 3 Strokes in every bar.

$\dfrac{4}{4}$ means 4 Strokes in every bar.

The lower figure denotes the time and the upper figures of time signs used in a bar as $\dfrac{2}{4}$ means 2 Signs of $\dfrac{1}{4}$ stroke in a bar.

Prolongation and Rest—They are also expressed by sign as:—

Whole rest — 4 Stroke rest.

Half rest — 2 Stroke rest.

Quarter rest — 1 Stroke rest.

$\dfrac{1}{8}$ rest — $\dfrac{1}{2}$ Stroke rest.

The pitch of the note is determined by its position in the Staff.

COMBINED NOTATION SYSTEM

(Indian and Foreign Notations).

This Combined Notation System is made to popularise the Indian music in Foreign countries. This system has been adopted in my books 'Learn To Play On Sitar, Guitar, Harmonium & Rag Asavari, (A Classical music book).

Before using combined notation system the musician should bear the following points in mind.

1. The middle points C is fixed for every song. Raga or tune as 'Sa' and this C note cannot be omitted. All the tunes are based on C note.

2. G note (P) cannot be changed in half tone or sharp notes.

3. P and F cannot be omitted at a time in any Raga.

Symbol of 1/4 matra of staff notation is accepted by our combined notation system equal to one matra time. Symbols of No. 1 and No. 2 are not used in combined notation system. The remaining fractional matra time symbols may be used as they are. The position of symbol of time notes in clef are accepted as they are.

Symbols of half tone notes and sharp note are accepted. The symbol of rest (—) is accepted for rest or prolonging the notes and not for stoppage. This symbol denotes one matra time. The symbol of prolonging notes for meend without dots are accepted as (--) and for combined notes as (—).

Combined Notation System

Full tone Notes—
Shudha swaras

S R G M P D N

Half tone notes—
Komal swaras.

G R D N

Sharp notes—
Tivra swara:

M

Lower octave notes   Medium Octave notes   Upper octave notes

E F C B   C D E F G A B C   D E F G A B C E
M P D N   S R G M P D N   S R G M P D N S R

Mandra saptak   Madhya saptak   Tar saptak

Combined notes in a matra time or more than two swaras in one matra time.

Stroke—
    Matra.

M M M M P M M P D

Matras Shown in Number. 1 2 3 4 5 6 etc. Ordinarily one note shows one matra time.

Tali Numbers are written on the bars.

Khali A Zero (0) is shown on the bar.

Sam A Sign of (+) is marked on the first matra of every Tala.

Khand (Bar)—Perpendicular lines are drawn for the parts of Talas.

Rest or prolonging the Notes a desh (—) marked after the Notes one desh shown one matra Time.

	Sam	Tali	Khali	Tali
	+	2	0	3
Matras	1 2 3 4	5 6 7 8	9 10 11 12	13 14 15 16